Emerging from the underbrush, I found myself in a grassy glade of some size which I had not seen before. And I knew I was traveling in the wrong direction, for I had not come this way, even in my hasty flight from the fangs of the sabertooth.

I was about to turn on my heel and strike out at random in another direction, when leaves rustled overhead.

In the next instant, the magnificent figure of a nearly naked black man swung from the branches above to land lightly as a cat on the emerald turf.

His bow was bent, the arrow nocked and ready. **Before I could think or move or speak, he loosed the deadly shaft directly for my heart!**

"He turned on his heel and sprinted."

ERIC
OF
ZANTHODON

Lin Carter

ILLUSTRATED BY
Josh Kirby

DAW Books, Inc.
Donald A. Wollheim, Publisher
1633 Broadway, New York, N.Y. 10019

DEDICATION:

To my favorite females in Fandom, Marilyn Halloran and Alina Chu . . . and to Cheryl, the real-life model for my "Niema."

FIRST PRINTING, MAY 1982

1 2 3 4 5 6 7 8 9

 DAW TRADEMARK REGISTERED
U.S. PAT. OFF. MARCA
REGISTRADA. HECHO EN U.S.A.

PRINTED IN U.S.A.

CONTENTS

IV. CROSSING THE ABYSS

V. SOLDIERS FROM YESTERDAY

VI. ERIC OF ZANTHODON

LIST OF ILLUSTRATIONS

WHAT HAS GONE BEFORE

Two explorers from the upper world, Eric Carstairs and Professor Potter, have penetrated into Zanthodon, the mysterious cavern-world beneath the trackless sands of the Sahara.

It is a strange and savage land, this Underground World, where gigantic beasts from forgotten ages roam, and dense jungles and swamps are home to many peoples—Cro-Magnon tribes and Neanderthal.

Befriended by the Cro-Magnon warriors, the adventurers have incurred the enmity of two powerful foes: Zarys, proud and beautiful Empress of a forgotten colony of Minoan Crete called the Scarlet City of Zar; and Kâiradine Redbeard, swaggering chief of the Barbary Pirates, who fled into the cavern-world of Zanthodon when driven from the seas of the Upper World many generations ago.

With both of these enemies on his trail, Eric Carstairs has succeeded in rescuing his beloved princess, Darya, from a thousand perils. Together with a host of Cro-Magnon fighting-men, they are on their way down the coast of the subterranean ocean which borders the savage land, seeking the faraway homeland of Darya and her people, the country of Thandar.

They are simultaneously attacked by the pirates and the legions of Zar, neither of whom has heretofore encountered the other. In the confusion of the battle, Kâiradine Redbeard mistakes the imperious Zarys for Darya, and carries her off, leaving her legions leaderless. Demoralized by the disappearance of their chief, the Barbary Pirates lose heart, and the Cro-Magnon tribes of Thandar and Sothar are victorious. Disarming their foes and leaving them to find their own way home to the pirate citadel of El-Cazar and the Scarlet City of Zar, Eric and the others continue through the mountains, searching for their southern homeland.

But young Jorn, a Thandarian hunter, and his sweetheart, Yualla of Sothar, have become lost. Pursuing his escaped hostages in hopes of recapturing them is wily, unscrupulous Xask, former vizier of the Empress and Eric's arch-enemy.

These three are absent during the final phase of the battle, as is whimpering, cowardly little Murg, who was forced by circumstances to accompany them as they made their escape.

Jorn, Yualla, Xask and Murg had vanished into the unknown at the conclusion of the fourth book of these adventures, a novel called *Darya of the Bronze Age*.

Their story is continued in these pages.

—*Lin Carter*

Waldenbooks

16 SALE   0529 0460/1   05/29/82

```
0553205315 3   1@   3.75        3.75
0879977310 3   1@   2.25        2.25

                    SUBTOTAL    6.00
TEXAS 5% TAX                     .30
                       TOTAL    6.30
                     PAYMENT    6.30

                      CHANGE     .00
```

THANK YOU - PLEASE COME AGAIN

05/29/82 12:38

PART ONE

The Fugitives

Chapter 1

THE HIDING PLACE

When the legions of Zar hurled themselves against the rear-most ranks of the corsairs, Jorn the Hunter found the moment he had been waiting for.

The Cro-Magnon boy gave Yualla the signal. Then he whirled, turning on the Zarian legionnaire assigned to guarding him, and kicked the astounded man in the stomach. As he sagged to his knees, gagging, the warrior could not have told which surprised him the most—the unexpected blow, or the fact that the hands of the youth were now free of their bonds.

In the same instant, Yualla had dispatched her own guard with her dagger. In the noise and tumult of battle, with the full attention of the Zarian warriors riveted on their foes, the Barbary Pirates, none but Murg noticed this burst of action.

Hastily stripping their guards of weapons, the boy and girl fled for safety behind tall boulders. From that vantage, they glided into thick bushes, seeking to circle the scene of battle and rejoin the tribe of Sothar from their rear.

As the two young people made their escape, Murg, who had been watching for just such an act, signaled to Xask, who was happy enough to have a reason to fall back into the rear. War was not one of Xask's favorite recreations. After all, people can get themselves killed when swords are flashing and spears are flying!

As Zarys led her legions into the fray, Xask prudently re-tired to a safer position, well out of the way of the flashing scimitars, the thrusting tridents. Accompanied by his entou-rage of personal guards, he initiated pursuit of the escaping hostages. Along the way, Murg and his guard fell into step with them, although Murg was no happier in battles than was Xask, and heartily wished himself far away from all these brave, bloody events.

Having no way of reading Xask's mind, then or now, I cannot say with certainty what motives urged the sly little

vizier to race in pursuit of the youth and maiden. Perhaps he
intended recapturing them, in order to trade their persons for
my old friend, the Professor, whose brain held the secret of
the thunder-weapon (as the folk of Zanthodon name my .45
automatic). Or perhaps he merely wished an excuse to put as
much distance between his tender hide and the furious battle
as could be done.

Jorn and Yualla, once safely out of the sight of their
former captors, took to their heels with alacrity. The handsome youth and his attractive blonde companion were young,
their lithe bodies toughened by the adventures through which
they had recently passed, and the Cro-Magnons are a hardy,
healthy people. Hence it was not long before they outdis-
tanced the men of Zar, who were smaller and less athletic
and who were, of course, burdened by their bronze armor
and heavy weapons.

The three-way battle between the Cro-Magnons, the Barbary Pirates, and the Zarians, had begun in an open,
meadowy space at the mouth of the pass which wound its
way through that soaring range of mountains known as the
Peaks of Peril. It is perhaps ironic that so many of our adventures had taken place in the vicinity of this ominously and
prophetically named range of mountains. The boy and girl
had intended to circle through the underbrush until they
reached the sheer and clifflike wall of the mountains, then
double back so as to rejoin their friends in the rear, where
they stood embattled with their backs set against the cliff.

Once Jorn's keen senses discovered that they were being
pursued by armed men, of course, his plans required swift al-
teration. The two struck out into the midst of the grassy
plain, hoping to evade their pursuers and probably, as well,
hoping that the Zarians would give over the pursuit when it
became impractical to continue it, and return to join their
comrades in the fighting.

The plains north of the mountains were level and feature-
less, and afforded the fugitives scant opportunities for
concealment. Once they had put a considerable distance between themselves and those that followed, it occurred to Jorn
the Hunter that they might manage to hide themselves in the
tall grasses. An act so obvious as that would not for long
have managed to confuse the warriors or huntsmen of his
own Cro-Magnon tribe, for of course they were seasoned
veterans, accustomed to the rough and hardy life of the wil-

derness and the jungle, who spent much of their lives tracking beasts through the woods in order to hunt and kill. Such as they could swiftly and easily have followed the trail left by the fugitives in the disturbed leaves and trampled grasses—as easily as you or I can peruse this printed page. But the Zarians were sophisticated city dwellers, no huntsmen, and to their dulled senses the trail left by the passage of Jorn and Yualla was all but invisible.

They had come to a shallow depression, where tall grass grew thick. It was here that the two sought to conceal themselves from their adversaries. It would have been but the action of mere moments for the two to crawl into the grasses, arranging the vegetation over them, and to lie still as rabbits seeking to evade the scrutiny of hawks.

Save for the unforeseen. . . .

Others had sought refuge in the shallow depression and had been hiding among the tall grasses, sensing the approach of tramping feet. These now exploded from their places of concealment, panicked by the two young people.

They were uld, small, edible, timid mammals resembling plump, diminutive deer. But deer they were not, for Professor Potter has identified them as eohippus, "dawn-horse," the remote ancestors of the modern animal.

Jorn snarled an oath, for the scattering uld would draw attention to their hiding place; and attention was the last thing he wished at the moment, with half a dozen armed Zarian legionnaires on their tracks.

Even as Jorn had feared, the flight of the uld had caught the eye of one of the Zarians. He started, pointing. Xask snapped a command and the guards fell into arrowhead formation, plowing through the high grass in the direction from which the herd of uld had fled in all directions.

And Xask smiled thinly: it was only a matter of moments now before the fugitives were found and became his captives once again.

Things have a way of falling out differently from what you may hope or expect, in Zanthodon as in the world above. But only in Zanthodon could the next twist of fate have occurred.

For other eyes had sighted the flight of the panic-stricken miniature horses. Those eyes belonged to an omodon, and a hungry brute of an omodon. Generally, such as the mighty cave-bear of the Ice Age lurk among the rocky crags of the Peaks of Peril, but the lust to gorge its empty belly on raw

red meat had driven this particular omodon down from the
heights, to prowl and hunt upon the plain.

The great bear had small, weak eyes, for which reason it
generally avoided the light of day, preferring the comfortable
gloom of the mountainside cave it had seized for its lair. But
its keen and sensitive nostrils more than made up for the
inadequacy of its vision, and it had sniffed the tasty uld upon
the wind.

The monster had been stealthily creeping through the tall
grass to where it had smelled out the hiding place of the herd
of uld. Now, as they exploded affrightedly in all directions, it
came roaring to its feet, mad with fury and frustration.

And when the mighty cave-bear of the Ice Age rises to its
full height, it is a fearsome thing to behold. Heavier and
higher than two grizzlies was the omodon, and its huge paws,
heavy as hammers, were armed with dreadful claws like
scythes.

And *this* was the adversary that came bellowing and lumbering down on the place where Jorn the Hunter and Yualla
of Sothar had sought to conceal themselves from danger and
discovery among the tall grasses!

Jorn sprang to his feet, clutching his small bronze dagger
futilely. It was, in fact, an imposing weapon filched from the
guard he had felled, and long enough to hold at bay a human
foe. But, against the giant bear that came lurching down upon
him, seemingly as huge as a hill, the blade seemed small and
useless. Nor was Yualla any better armed; now had both the
youth and the maid good reason to regret not having taken
up the spears their guards had let fall.

At the time, they had hastily reasoned the cumbersome
weapons were too large and clumsy to be safely borne in
flight.

Now they wished they had thought twice about that.

But now, of course, it was too late.

Chapter 2

AT THE BOATS

Intent on punishing the blond savages whom she believed to be the same host of barbarians that had earlier defeated her upon the great plains of the north, Zarys of Zar led her mailed legions forward at the charge, and assaulted the rear ranks of the Barbary Pirates who were also attacking the Cro-Magnons.

Who these other adversaries were, the Divine Zarys neither knew nor cared to know. It sufficed for the imperious and prideful young woman that they were in her way.

Her well-disciplined legions carved their way through the rear of the buccaneers, who scattered in all directions in surprise and consternation. The corsairs fell before the thrusting spears and tridents of the Zarian legion in the dozen and the score. In less time than it takes to tell, the Empress had cut a red path into the very heart of the strange, swarthy men who wore such curious and ridiculous garments.

As she did so, she came to the attention of Kâiradine Redbeard, who stopped fighting and stared at her with open mouth. She was certainly worth staring at, was Zarys of Zar: supple, half-naked, slim and lovely, her fiercely lovely face crowned with a curling mass of golden hair, her wonderful body clad in strangely shaped bits of gold-washed armor. High greaves, worked with scenes of the hunt and war, adorned her slender, graceful legs; a breastplate, cunningly molded to fit her figure, clad her high breasts and shielded her belly, and it was carven with mythological events and monsters. A sparkling, jeweled coronet completed her riding costume.

But it was not the stunning beauty of the ravishing girl that seized the astounded eye of the Redbeard, but the fact that he instantly recognized her as Darya, the jungle princess for whom he had conceived so violent a passion as to pursue her in her flight to this very scene of battle.

I have elsewhere remarked upon the fact that the Empress of Zar bore an amazing resemblance to my beloved Princess,

17

despite the fact that they came of different races. Indeed, upon first laying eyes upon the Divine Empress of the Scarlet City, I myself had mistaken her for my darling Darya. So it is quite understandable that Kâiradine Redbeard made the same mistaken assumption.

He flung himself upon her without a moment's hesitation, battering down her blade and seizing her lithe and supple body in his strong arms.

While he struggled to subdue the astounded and, naturally, infuriated young woman, Kâiradine directed his personal retinue of well-armed corsairs to engage the guards from whose midst he had seized Zarys. These were quickly dispatched.

The midst of a battle was no place to try to take captives, and had Kâiradine been less madly desirous of the girl he held in his arms, this might have occurred to him. But the Prince of the Barbary Pirates felt a violent and consuming lust for Darya of Thandar, and heretofore—quite maddeningly—she had managed to evade his embraces. Now that he had her at last, the farthest thing from his mind was to let her go.

When, exhausted, Zarys finally ceased struggling against him, the Redbeard swiftly bound and gagged the young woman. Then, turning abruptly to the amazed Moustapha, his second-in-command, who had watched these actions without comprehension, he curtly directed his lieutenant to take what actions he could to hold the corsair lines firm against their adversaries.

Without waiting for a reply, the Redbeard turned and began cutting his way through the confused and milling battle toward the distant beach where his longboats lay concealed.

In the whirling chaos into which the three-way battle had degenerated, he vanished from the knowledge of men and was gone, leaving the unhappy Moustapha to strive to hold together a rapidly deteriorating situation, which soon because quite hopeless.

It had probably been in Kâiradine's mind to leave his captive bound and helpless in the boats, returning to take command again. And here you see demonstrated one of the disadvantages of inditing a factual narrative, a difficulty not usually faced by the authors of mere fiction. This is, I have no way of knowing what was in the Redbeard's mind and am only reconstructing the sequence of events from information which has come to me long after these events took place.

At length he reached that stretch of sandy shore bordering a swampy area, where pools of stagnant water were thickly grown with mangrove trees whose long and frondlike branches formed a veil of leafage. Here it was the corsairs had dragged their longboats up the beach to a place of hiding in the edges of the marsh, among the heavy shrubbery. They had chopped down with their cutlasses long palmlike leaves to drape across the boats, further concealing them from chance discovery.

And when he reached this place, the Prince of the Barbary Pirates found an unwelcome and unpleasant surprise awaiting him.

This beach formed part of the shores of the Sogar-Jad, as the subterranean sea was known to the Zanthodonians. And the waves of that steamy ocean are filled with innumerable varieties of marine life, dominant among which are the great aquatic saurians of Earth's remotest dawn age.

Those who have perused the earlier volumes of these memoirs will recall the ferocious yith, or plesiosaur, which inhabits the depths of the Sogar-Jad. This monstrous reptile, and veritable double for the famous Sea Serpent of legend, had intervened in these adventures on two previous occasions. Most recently, one had attacked the flagship of Kâiradine himself, nearly biting off the right arm of the Redbeard.*

The monster which Kâiradine found browsing among the boats with no yith. It was seven times the size of the plesiosaur! Like a moving mountain of glistening, leathery flesh it was, with its slick hide covered with scaly excrescences and a neck long enough to top the tallest of the prehistoric conifers which lined the edge of the sandy beach.

Had Professor Potter been present, I imagine that the scrawny little savant would have identified the lumbering monstrosity as none other than the brontosaurus itself, the largest mammal that ever walked the world.

The Zanthodonians refer to the giant reptile as the gorgorog. I had yet to encounter a member of its species during my own travels and adventures through this prehistoric world, for they are few and but seldom encountered by men. The men of Zar had domesticated a smaller, lighter variety of the brontosaurus, which they call the thodar. But this was

---

* You will find this scene described at length in the fourth volume of these books, a novel entitled *Darya of the Bronze Age*.

surely no thodar! It would have taken three of the smaller brutes to make up the huge bulk of this moving mountain.

Kâiradine shrank into the shelter of the trees, snarling Moslem curses. The Prince of the Barbary Pirates was no coward, but even his curved saber of shining Damascus steel would be as useless as a wisp of grass against six hundred tons of meat and muscle.

The reptile, unknown to Kâiradine, was no meat-eater but a vegetarian. It lumbered through the shallows on four legs thicker about than treetrunks, dipping its blunt-nosed head into the tidal pools, gulping and munching seaweed and other marine growths, as mild and harmless as a browsing milk cow.

As it lumbered through the marshy places, however, its huge and ponderous feet had heedlessly trampled into matchwood three of the longboats, and others had been dislodged from their moorings and were floating out to sea.

Kâiradine was in a quandary! He could hardly leave Zarys in one of the boats, so near to the giant reptile. Greatly daring, he might have gained one of the boats and rowed out to sea, where his ship lay at anchor. But the gorgorog was too close to the boats for him to attempt this.

What, then, to do?

The Redbeard narrowed his eyes, staring thoughtfully about. He noticed how the lazy washing of the waves caused the loose boats to drift to and fro. The tides were not strong enough at this point along the shore to suck them out to sea. . . .

I have never exactly understood why the underground ocean had tides at all, since, surely, the attraction of the moon as it waxed and waned could exert no influence on a body of water miles beneath the planet's crust. Perhaps that the Sogar-Jad had tides at all, no matter how slight, was due to centrifugal force, caused by the Earth as it revolved upon its axis.

I do not know, and this is no place to inquire into such arcane matters. But one of the boats, freed of its mooring, had been carried a ways off down the shore, and lay floating in the shallows some considerable distance away from where the huge lumbering gorgorog browsed.

Kâiradine transferred his wriggling feminine burden to one broad shoulder, and crept through the trees, emerging from the cover of the trees at the point where the floating longboat was closest to the shoreline.

I suppose it was the plan of the Pirate Prince to board the boat, deposit his wriggling burden aft, and row her out to where the Barbary ship was anchored.

It was as good a plan as Kâiradine could have devised, given the circumstances.

But not quite good enough.

For the stealthy figure of the turbaned corsair with the half-naked blonde woman across one shoulder caught the glazed, indifferent eye of the brontosaurus.

Through what passed for its brain—a miniscule, atrophied organ probably no longer than a peanut—there flickered a gleam of idle curiosity.

Doubtless, never before in all its days had the monster reptile seen a bearded, swarthy man in brilliantly colorful silk pantaloons slinking along the beach with a struggling golden-haired woman across one shoulder and a saber flashing in one gemmed fist.

Mild wonderment entered the gaze of the placid reptile. Its endless appetite momentarily lulled to repletion by the sea-salad which had served as its luncheon, the brontosaurus decided to investigate. A casual stroll along the beach, after all, is good for the digestion after a hearty meal.

Over his shoulder, Kâiradine looked and saw the great lumbering monster heading for him. Growling a curse, he turned on his heel and sprinted farther up the beach, away from where the empty long-boat bobbed up and down, so tantalizingly close.

At a leisurely pace, which shook the ground underfoot only slightly, the six-hundred-ton dinosaur followed inquiringly.

Soon both the pursuer and the pursued were far down the beach and out of sight.

Chapter 3.

HUROK HAS A PROBLEM

While these things had been taking place, the battle had collapsed into a vast, noisy mob of confused, bewildered, leaderless men—in which only the Cro-Magnon warriors managed to keep their wits about them and press their advantage.

The corsairs had lost many of their number while trying to attack from the front and defend themselves from the rear. When Kâiradine Redbeard had vanished from their midst, many had lost heart and prudently flung down their weapons to take to their heels. Moustapha could do little or nothing about this, since even the leader of a host cannot be everywhere at once.

As for the Zarian legion, once their impetuous Empress had hurled herself into the van, only to disappear as if the earth had opened to swallow her up, they, too, fell into a demoralized disarray, which was only aggravated further with the discovery that the second-in-command, the nefarious Xask, had also mysteriously disappeared.

The Cro-Magnon tribe, augmented by the timely arrival of mighty Tharn of Thandar and his own host of warriors, found little difficulty in achieving the victory. The Barbary Pirates and the men of the lost colony of Minoan Crete, already deserting in droves, now flung down their weapons and sullenly surrendered.

Garth of Sothar and Tharn of Thandar, not wishing to needlessly encumber themselves with such a host of prisoners, simply confiscated and surrendered arms and let the captives go. Perhaps the defeated warriors would fall prey to the monstrous prehistoric beasts that roamed the wilderness, perhaps they would, after long wanderings, manage to find their way safely back again to their homelands. That was up to them, and, for their part, the Pirates and the Zarians departed hastily from the scene of their defeat.

The women and children, the aged and the injured, the twin tribes had sent through the mountain pass to the relative safety of the southern plains. Now heavily armed with sophisticated weapons of edged metal taken from the Barbary Pirates and the men of Zar, the fighting men of the tribes wasted no time in crossing the Peaks of Peril and rejoining those that had gone before.

We made our camp on the plains of the south and rested and ate and took care of our wounds. Also, the chieftains conferred in council as to future courses of action.

"With the recovery of the gomad Darya, your daughter, my brother," said Garth of Sothar, "no further reason exists to keep you and yours from returning to your homeland."

Tharn solemnly agreed. He said: "My only remaining wish could be that your own daughter, the gomad Yualla, had survived the perils of the north, so that you could rejoice in the recovery of your child as I do in the recovery of my own."

Garth thanked his fellow monarch for the sentiment, and said nothing further on this subject. At this time, my reader will understand, none of us had any way of knowing that Yualla still lived, or that young Jorn the Hunter had survived his dive into the mountain lake.

Once we were fed and rested and had bound our wounds, we departed, to cross the plain and enter the jungles. As explained earlier in these memoirs, the tribe of Sothar were homeless, for their country had been devastated by earthquake and volcanic eruption, precipitating them into hasty flight, followed by long wanderings. The two tribes had joined together out of a desire for the mutual protection afforded by numbers; since then, they had become close friends, and Tharn had offered them room in his country for their living places, for the forested plains of Thandar were broad and much land lay empty.

So the host that headed south into the jungles was far more numerous than the host that had originally marched north on the trail of the lost Princess Darya.

And to this number had also been added the many slaves who had fled with the Professor and me when the mad god, Zorgazon, had destroyed the Scarlet City of Zar.* These were men taken by the Zarian slavers from other scattered Cro-Magnon tribes which inhabited the little-known northern

---

* The titanic Zorgazon, a tyrannosaurus rex, demolished the city of Zar in scenes described in the third volume of these memoirs a book entitled *Hurok of the Stone Age*.

parts of the subterranean continent. Tharn and Garth had offered them a place among us, which they had gratefully
accepted.

Several of them, in fact, had volunteered to join my own
company of warriors, for I had become a chieftain high in
the councils of the twin tribes. Among these were my stalwart
friends, cheerful, merry-hearted Thon of Numitor and that
stolid but faithful giant, Gundar of Gorad, who had become
my friends during the time we were penned up in the Pits of
Zar, awaiting the Great Games of the God.

Also among my company were gallant Varak and his mate,
Ialys of Zar, who had fled with us, and Grond of Gorthak
and little Jaira, his mate, who had been slaves in the island
fortress of El-Cazar. These, together with the other warriors
of my company, such as mighty Hurok of Kor, had swelled
the numbers in my service until we jestingly described ourselves as a miniature tribe, not just a company.

Each company seeks its own camping place, and lights its
own cook-fires, and marches together. Hence, as we entered
the edges of the jungle, we were a little apart from the others
and forced to make our own path through the dense undergrowth and heavy foliage.

I was in the lead, of course, with Hurok the Neanderthal
on my right hand, and Gundar on my left. The Cro-Magnon
gladiator was the only panjani (as the Neanderthal Apemen
of Kor refer to us) who could compare, in bulk and breadth
of shoulder, in sheer physical might, to my old comrade
Hurok, and venturing into the jungle I felt more comfortable
with these two stalwarts at my side.

These jungles have many denizens, and among them are
some of the most feared and savage beasts that ever roamed
the upper world, the lumbering grymp, or triceratops, the
vandar, as the Cro-Magnons name the dreaded sabertooth tiger, and the goroth (or prehistoric bull, known as the aurochs
to science) are among these, and not the least among them,
as you can imagine.

But the commotion made by the entry into the jungle
country of such a host of warriors and their women, number-
ing over a thousand by now, drove even the more ferocious
predators into hiding—a fact for which we all had cause to
be thankful.

Still and all, we trod the jungle aisles warily, senses alert
for the slightest sign of danger, weapons bared and ready in

After a time, I began to notice that Hurok seemed unusually somber and silent, even for one given to few words. I glanced at the burly form of my friend curiously. Finally I spoke up.

"Why are you so silent, Hurok?" I asked. "Is anything bothering you in particular?"

"There is a certain matter on Hurok's mind," admitted the Apeman of Kor in his slow, deep voice, "but naught that concerns his friend Black Hair."

"Anything that worries the mind of Hurok, worries his friend Black Hair," I said. "For Black Hair and Hurok of Kor are more than friends: they are brothers."

A gleam of pleasure momentarily brightened the small, dull eyes, buried under heavy neanderthaloid brow-ridges. Then it was gone, but I knew it for his version of a smile.

"Perhaps at a later time," he said heavily, "Hurok the Drugar will apprise Black Hair the panjani of that which is in his heart."

I was troubled by these words, and did not like the sound of them. For one thing, "Drugar" is the word by which the Cro-Magnons call the Apeman of Kor, and it is more or less to be considered a derogatory term. "Panjani" is the word the Apemen of Kor use for the Cro-Magnons: it means "smooth-skins."

It bothered me that Hurok employed these terms. I could remember earlier occasions when he found himself unwelcome among the fighting men of Thandar because of his race, which they have good reason to detest. Neanderthal and Cro-Magnon have been at war since their remotest ancestors found their way into the hidden cavern world of Zanthodon, and they remain blood foes to this day. But Hurok had long since earned the respect and the friendship of the Cro-Magnon comrades by whose side he had fought many battles and braved the perils of the wilderness.

I said nothing more, assuming that in his own good time, my huge, hairy friend would unburden his heart to me.

And made thereby a mistake I later had cause to regret. . . . one, if I may say so, among very many!

The misty-golden skies of Zanthodon know neither sun nor moon, neither night nor day. A perpetual late-afternoon light illuminates the humid atmosphere of the Underground World, under the vast curve of its cavernous roof. This mysterious luminescence, which derives neither from sun nor moon nor stars, is belived to be caused by some chemical action akin to phosphorescence.

Lacking sun and moon, the men and women of Zanthodon know neither day nor night. Unaware of these divisions of time, they tend to sleep whenever they become sleepy, and to awaken when they are sufficiently rested.

After we had cut our way through the thick jungles below the plain of the thantors* for what must have been many hours, weariness overcame us, and the desire for sleep.

Each company of warriors chose its own ground and posted its own sentinels. Hurok volunteered to take the first watch, with no particular reason; I think I assumed the glum old fellow wished to be alone with his thoughts.

When we awoke, he was gone.

---

* So called because of the famous stampede of the herd of thantors, or woolly mammoths, which occurred on those plains, in which the host of the Apemen of Kor was virtually destroyed. See the first volume of this series, *Journey to the Underground World.*

Chapter 4.

XASK RUNS INTO TROUBLE

When the great cave bear came rearing up on its hind legs and burst into a lumbering charge, Jorn and Yualla sprang from their places of concealment in the tall grass.

Since there was no way of fighting the monster with the weapons they held, their only recourse lay in flight. For the Cro-Magnon youngsters were young and lithe and swift-footed, and could easily outrun the shaggy ponderous brute.

Instinctively, they took opposite directions so as to confuse the beast and make him pause to consider which fleeing youngster to pursue. Not looking back, they raced off into the plain.

The omodon paused uncertainly, peering with small, weak eyes after the two escaping morsels, growling hungrily, trying to make up what passed for its mind.

This was the scene which confronted Xask and Murg and the six guards when they came pelting up to the spot from which the uld had scattered. The Zarians came to a stumbling halt, staring at the shaggy monster. At its full height, the omodon towered twenty feet high, and seemed a veritable ogre to the small slightly-built legion warriors. Spying them, it opened an enormous fanged maw, roared its angry challenge, and came charging down upon them with an earth-shaking stride.

In no time it was among them, hammer-heavy paws batting them aside. One guard went flying, his skull shattered. Another staggered back, pawing at the gory ruin of its face, slashed to ribbons with one swipe of the bear's huge, fearsomely armed paw. A third screamed and fell, disemboweled at a stroke.

Only one guard stood and faced the lumbering hill of fury muscle that came thundering down upon him. He thrust with a lightning-swift stroke, sinking the keen points of his metal trident in the bear's belly. Instead of felling or even slowing the cave-bear, the wound only seemed to infuriate him.

27

He caught up the guard in the grip of those great paws.
And bit his head off.

That was enough for Xask! Without further ado, watching his guards fall before the angry brute, the prudent vizier turned and took to his heels.

Murg hovered indecisively, squeaking, licking dry lips with a dry tongue. Then he took off in the same direction Xask had taken. A tall stand of trees stood in the midst of the plain, some distance away; it was the only thing in sight that might afford a safe haven, and toward it Xask had instinctively fled.

Murg followed.

Seeing its fleet-footed prey vanish in the distance, the bear grunted sourly. It quickly dispatched the last of the guards, then squatted on its hunkers to regard the gore-splashed corpses strewn and sprawled about amid the trampled grasses.

Most bears in the upper world prefer fat grubs, insects or leafy vegetation. The great cave-bear of the Ice Age, however, was less fussy in its tastes, and had developed a hearty fondness for raw meat.

Dragging the nearer corpse over to where it squatted, the bear sniffed at the bloody thing. It vastly preferred the timid, tasty uld—man-meat was stringy and sour. Still and all, hunters cannot be choosers.

It began to feed. . . .

After about an hour, Yualla caught up with Jorn, having left the omodon far behind, finishing its meal. Neither of the young people was even winded by the rapid pace they had maintained across the plain, but it was good to pause and rest a little. They found a sheltered pool, nestled in the shoulder of one of the foothills of the Peaks of Peril, and satisfied their thirst therein.

Their flight from the cave-bear had carried them far into the midst of the plain, where it bordered the range of gray peaks. They were, in fact, near to the point at which the mountains petered out, diminishing into hills and hummocks.

While they rested, they discussed the situation.

"There is no point in retracing our steps to the scene of battle, for by this time our people have either won or lost the contest," remarked Jorn thoughtfully.

"They will have sent the women and children, the aged and the injured, through the pass to the safety of the far side of the mountains," Yualla said.

"It would be a lot easier to circle the end of the range here and rejoin the survivors on the other side," murmured Jorn.

Yualla agreed with his choice of actions. Taking up their weapons, the two Cro-Magnon youngsters began making their way through the foothills at the end of the mountain range. They traced a path through narrow, rocky defiles, a mazelike labyrinth, which consumed much more time than it should.

Jorn and Yualla were alert for danger. These mountains were the haunts of many dangerous beasts, among whom the omodon was but one. Sabertooth tigers made their rocky lairs in the flanks of the mountains, and upon the summit of the peaks thakdols nested.

Having once been carried off by a hungry thakdol, Yualla had no particular wish to repeat the experience.

The thakdol is the bat-winged flying reptile the scientists of the Upper World call the pterodactyl, so you can imagine how the cavegirl felt.

The Peaks of Peril, you see, were aptly named. . . .

Whatever gods watch over the wandering adventurers of Zanthodon seemed to have taken the Cro-Magnon couple under their care, for despite the numerous savage denizens of the Peaks of Peril, Jorn and Yualla encountered no further dangers during their journey through the hills.

Before the world was very much older, they found themselves on the southern side* of the mountains, and saw before them the broad and level plain of the thantors, and, beyond these, the dark edges of the jungle country.

For a time they went along the flanks of the mountains, heading back in the direction from which they had fled. At length weariness overcame them and they prepared to sleep. They had also, by this time, developed hearty appetites— young Cro-Magnons being no different in that wise than the young people of the Upper World.

Since no game surfaced to visibility, there was nothing to do about their hunger except to attempt to forget it and seize the opportunity to sleep.

---

* Eric Carstairs adds a footnote here, to the effect that the compass directions are unknown in the Underground World, but in order to make clear the directions of travel, he adopted an arbitrary system of his own devising. Thandar lay to the south, the Sogar-Jad to the west, and the Scarlet City of Zar to the east. At the moment, Jorn and Yualla are in the north.

Finding a cozy nook among the rocks, they rolled up the long, dry grasses into a soft bed, and composed themselves for slumber.

Jorn was acutely aware of Yualla's nearness. He had fallen in love with the pretty Cro-Magnon maid during their adventures together, and young blood ran hot in his healthy body. But he tried to ignore the tempting nearness and pretend he did not feel the desires that surged within him.

The Cro-Magnons, our remote ancestors, enjoyed a simpler and less complicated code of behavior than the cumbersome system of laws and restrictions our modern urban civilization imposes. They bare their bodies before members of the opposite sex indifferently, uncaringly, but when they mate it is a serious commitment for life.

Hence Jorn's forbrearance and, also, his discomfort.

Perhaps it would have comforted him to know that Yualla was every bit as aware of his own nearness as he was of hers. Nor did she ache the less to feel his arms about her and his lips upon her own.

The two spent an uncomfortable night.

I use the word to simplify the need for explanations. In a world without sun or moon, a world bathed in perpetual day, there is no such condition as night.

Jorn awoke first and lay very still and remained quiet. Sensing her companion, against whose naked body she lay nestled, Yualla roused herself, yawned hugely, stretched, and asked him how he had slept.

When he did not at once answer, she rolled over and looked at him. And quickly understood the reason for his silence.

It is hard to speak with the point of a long spear just tickling your Adam's apple. . . .

Chapter 5.

KÂIRADINE HAS A BAD DAY

Kâiradine looked distinctly unhappy, and indeed the Prince of El-Cazar *was* extremely unhappy. So would you have been, had you been misfortunate enough to have been in his predicament.

It is bad enough being chased by an inquisitive dinosaur, but it is even worse being treed by one. For the better part of an hour, the enormous brontosaurus had lumbered about the sandy beach, mildly curious as to what had become of the peculiar man-things she had followed all this way. It never occurred to the dim intelligence of the monstrous herbivore to look into the treetops: had she done so, she would have observed the hapless Redbeard uncomfortably straddling a branch, but she* did not.

His gorgeous silken pantaloons were ripped and torn by the rough bark of the trunk he had so hastily climbed. His turbaned headdress had been knocked askew when his head collided with a branch he had not noticed.

To make it worse, it had begun to rain.

The sudden showers of Zanthodon are warm, for the climate is mild; also, they are quickly over. You get just as wet and miserable from them, however, as when you are caught in the rains of the Upper World.

To make things even less comfortable for the buccaneer, the drenching rains had made the red dye which stained his trim, small fringe of beard run, and the reddish stuff was trickling down his throat to stain his shirt.

As for Zarys, who sat side-saddle on the next branch, the Divine Empress of Zar had seldom gone through such a heady variety of violent emotions in so brief a time.

First there had been the unheard-of experience of having

---

* I have no idea why Eric Carstairs chose to refer to the huge gorgorog by the feminine pronoun, but it could hardly have been from any personal knowledge of "her" gender!

the tall leader of the corsair host fling himself so unexpectedly upon her, crushing her in his arms, and carrying her off,
bound and helpless and in a fury such as the gorgeous young
woman had never known. Incredulity stung her to venomous
rage. *Never* in all of the years of her young life had the
Sacred Empress of the Scarlet City been so rudely handled by
a mere man—that he had dared attack her in the first place
was amazing enough, but to have trussed her like a roped
uld, tossed her across one broad shoulder, and carried her off
into the wilderness was a lese majesté beyond description.

There was little or nothing she could have done about it at
the moment, of course, although she struggled like an infuriated leopardess in the prison of his brawny arms, snarling im-
precations, spitting curses, and uttering imperious commands
which went completely ignored and which were, in fact, soon
quite effectively cut off by the sudden imposition of a gag.

To make matters worse, all the while, obviously enjoying
the pressure of her warm and supple, half-naked body against
his own, the Redbeard had grinned down exultantly at his
beautiful, if furious, and very helpless, captive. . . .

But now the Empress had gone from one extreme to another. If it was insulting and outrageous to be carried off like
a slave girl by the corsair, it was distinctly less pleasant to be
forced to climb a tall tree in order to escape the unwelcome
attentions of the most enormous reptile she had ever seen,
this side of Zorgazon himself, her co-divinity and, technically,
her "mate."

Now, panting, disheveled, soaked to the skin, weary from
her exertions, she clung to the branch and endured the downpour as best she could.

At least, her hands and legs were free of their bonds; that
was *one* good thing about her present uncomfortable predicament! Strong as he was, with his newly healed shoulder,
Kâiradine Redbeard could hardly have climbed the tree encumbered by one hundred and fifteen pounds of furiously
struggling woman. So he had cut her bonds and urged her up
the trunk ahead of him at sword-point.

By this time, it had become perfectly obvious to the Pirate
Prince that he had carried off the wrong girl. Not that the
voluptuous descendant of the ancient monarchs of Crete was
not worth carrying off, of course: it was simply that she was
not Darya, although her resemblance to the Cro-Magnon girl
was incredible.

For one thing, Kâiradine knew that the savage tribes which

inhabited the Underground World—Cro-Magnon and Neanderthal alike—share in common the same universal tongue I have called Zanthodonian. Only the Zarians and the Barbary Pirates have languages of their own: the Zarians speak an obsolete, classical form of the little-known ancient Minoan tongue, while the corsairs converse in a debased form of Arabic.

Never before having encountered any of the people of the Scarlet City, the Pirate Prince had no idea what language it was that Zarys was cursing him in. But he knew that Darya of Thandar could speak only in Zanthodonian, so this could not be she.

Also, he had discovered to his surprise that the young woman was bald as an egg!

Her golden hair was thus revealed as naught but a wig of spun gold wire, which had been knocked askew as had his own turban by collision with the same unseen branch.

All in all, it just had not been Kâiradine's day. . . .

In time, things got a little better. For one thing, the rains stopped as abruptly as they had begun. For another, the great bronto had forgotten about the humans it had pursued out of harmless and idle curiosity, and went lumbering off in search of a second helping of sea-salad, dragging its huge and heavy tail behind it.

They clambered down the tree and stood there for a moment, looking at each other.

Kâiradine had never seen a woman clad in gold-washed armor and jeweled coronet—a woman who acted so imperiously as this one, being accustomed to harem women and tavern wenches. He looked her over puzzledly, rather liking what he saw.

For her part, Zarys had never encountered a man anything like Kâiradine Redbeard before, either, and she was looking him up and down with much the same curiosity.

He was lean and dark-skinned, this descendent of Desert Hawks and the Wolves of the Sea, and taller than the men of Zar, with an impressive musculature and long legs, wolfishly handsome with his aquiline nose and brilliant eyes.

He was quite a lot of man, was Kâiradine; a black-hearted villain, of course, but still . . . quite a lot of man. Zarys was intrigued in spite of herself. Accustomed from childhood to cringing and servile courtiers—all oily flattery and seductive gallantries—she rather liked the looks of this hard, rangy is-

land princeling, with his unfamiliar but colorful raiment and
sheer virility. He was *so* unlike the men she had always
known . . . !

"Well?" she snapped, after a good long look. "Are you going to stand there gawking at me? Why did you carry me
off—where are we—what are your intentions—where are you
going—and what are you going to do?"

A bit dazed by the directness of this torrent of inquiries,
the Redbeard hemmed and hawed a bit, trying to figure out
just what he *was* going to do. He stared up and down the
beach, striving to remember from which direction he had
come. The tide had erased his footprints by now, and the rain
had finished up the job. Also, he had turned this way and
that, back-tracking and circling about, dashing hither and
yon, crawling into thickets, hiding in tall grasses, all in a vain
attempt to shake the pursuing brontosaurus off their trail. But
the inquisitive, if slow-thinking, monster reptile had simply
come lumbering on, refusing to become confused.

Anyway, all this running about and doubling back and so
on—while it had not managed to confuse the inquisitive saurian—had certainly gotten Kâiradine Redbeard confused, to
such an extent that he could not at once with any certainty
reckon his present position in relation to the whereabouts of
his embattled corsairs or his ship. Strain his hawk-sharp eyes
as he might, he could see no sign of the corsair vessel. Either
he had run a greater distance than he had first assumed, or it
could not be seen because of the misty, humid atmosphere.

It did not at once occur to Kâiradine that his men,
slouching back from the battle in which they had suffered so
humiliating a defeat, had found the surviving boats and
rowed back to their ship and sailed away for El-Cazar.

I suspect this was the case, for we never ran into the Barbary Pirates again, but I do not really know.

The Empress seated herself on a fallen log, straightened
her golden wig, and crossed her arms upon her perfect
breasts, eyeing the Barbary Pirate with an aloof and lofty expression.

"We are hungry," she informed him coolly.

Well, so was Kâiradine, by that time. He looked about in a
determined but helpless fashion. Dirk and dagger and slim saber of Damascus steel were his only weapons, useless for
slaying seafowl or bringing down a plump uld. He began to
scout around for sustenance.

He was quite unhappy.

In time, with a disdainful sniff, Zarys deigned to join him in the food-shopping. It was Zarys who found the seaside nest of the zomak, or archeopteryx, filled with large, succulent and unhatched eggs. It was also Zarys who found clams and other edible shellfish in a tidal pool. All that the Redbeard was able to come up with was a few ripe fruits, berries, and a handful of nuts which the Empress disdained as too green to eat.

They made a fire in a hole dug in the beach, cooked the eggs and boiled the shellfish in a hollow gourd full of saltwater. They munched this crude repast moodily, and Kâiradine gamely and stubbornly chewed and swallowed down the green nuts which Zarys had rejected.

After this scant meal, weariness overcame them. They went to sleep in the bushes, Zarys careful to keep well apart from the Barbary Prince.

They slept.

Kâiradine awoke in acute discomfort, discovering that the woman had been right, after all: the nuts *were* too green to be safely eaten.

He trotted down the beach a ways and was noisily sick into the sand. Not yet asleep, Zarys smiled a catlike smile of deep, feminine satisfaction to hear him at it, then curled up cozily and fell into a deep, refreshing slumber.

It served him right. . . .

PART TWO

The Black Amazon

Chapter 6.

NIEMA THE AZIRU

The spear which just touched the throat of Jorn the Hunter was in itself curious, a smooth, tapering shaft of fire-hardened wood, very unlike the flint or bronze-bladed spears used by the Cro-Magnons, but the person holding the spear was so remarkable in appearance that it was she who seized and held their amazed attention.

She was naked, save for sandals of tough stegosaurus hide, and a narrow strip of hide worn low on her slim hips and wound between her thighs, leaving belly, buttocks and thighs quite bare. Save for these, and a rude necklace of animal fangs strung about her throat on a thong, she was completely naked.

Her skin was black as polished ebony and she stood two inches over six feet in height, with broad shoulders, a lean waist, narrow hips and long, exquisitely shaped legs. Exquisite, too, were her naked breasts, pointed and thrusting and flawless in their rondures as ripe fruit.

But it was the color of her skin that amazed the blond boy and girl. Never before had they seen or even heard of someone with skin as black as ink, and the novelty of the hue intrigued and fascinated them.

She had a lovely face poised atop a long neck, and her features were subtly different from those of the Cro-Magnons. Her brow was high and round, her hair closely braided to her scalp in corn-row style, and copper bangles hung from the lobes of her small ears. Her nose was small, her upper lip long, her mouth wide, mobile, full-lipped. She was stunningly beautiful in a new, exciting way.

She regarded the two warily, her expression ominous, her brilliant and expressive dark eyes studying them carefully. Eventually, she lowered the assegai until its needle point touched the boy's chest above his heart.

Niema the Aziru had lived in the eastern part of these mountains for some weeks now, without seeing another human being, and she had come upon the sleeping pair unexpectedly. Her first instinct had been to protect herself by taking the initiative; now, she realized they were as astounded to discover her in this place as she had been when she stumbled upon them. Nor did they look like the advance guard of a migrating Cro-Magnon tribe, as she had feared at first.

In fact, they looked to her like savage sweathearts who had run away from their tribal grounds to be alone together. And the way the boy's strong arm went protectively about the girl's slim shoulders, while she nestled her cheek against his breast, gave further evidence of this. Her alert gaze softened and her full lips widened in a smile, revealing flawless teeth of snowy white.

"I am Niema," she said in a husky voice, "and my people are the Aziru tribe. Who are you, and why are you alone here in this mountainous wilderness, where very little water is to be found, but very many dangerous beasts roam and hunt? Are you lost—or runaways—or fugitives?"

Jorn the Hunter was much relieved that he was not going to be stuck with the long spear which the strange black woman held and wielded so knowledgeably, before he had an opportunity to speak.

"I am Jorn, a hunter of the tribe of Thandar, and this girl is the gomad Yualla of Sothar, the daughter of the High Chief," he explained boldly. Then he added: "She is under the protection of Jorn the Hunter!"

The young black woman suppressed a grin at this, and listened seriously as the Cro-Magnon boy briefly explained how and why they had come to be here.

"We have been held captive by a people who dwell far away in the north," said Jorn the Hunter. "We managed to break away and were seeking our own people, who are encamped not very distant from here, when weariness overtook us. We are not your enemies."

"And would be your friends, if you will let us," added Yualla demurely. Privately, she found Niema fascinating to look upon and was instantly curious to know her better.

Niema spread long-fingered hands in an eloquent shrug and put away her assegai. Squatting comfortably upon her heels she told them about herself and her people.

There were facts that Niema did not know, and her sense of the passing of time was hazy, so I will interpolate here her story and the story of her people as we later pieced it together, rather than keep my readers mystified.

The Aziru tribe had formerly inhabited the great veldt to the south of the Sahara Desert, beneath whose sandy vastness lay the Underground World. Driven from their grazing grounds when famine had decimated their herds, they wandered north, led by a visionary chief named Imre, to whom the Ancestors spoke in his dreams. In time, the survivors of the tribe found their way down into Zanthodon through one of the numerous volcanic fumeroles which gave entry into the gigantic cavern world.

They found the plains of the thantors to their liking, and, far to the east of those portions of the plains we had seen and visited, built their huts and erected their palisade of sharpened stakes. In this kraal, the remnants of the Aziru lived for what Niema referred to as "nearly seven generations."

Professor Potter believes the Aziru took refuge in the Underground World no more than a hundred years ago, when many of the black tribes of North Africa were in turmoil. Niema's concept of time is based on generations from mother to daughter; and a generation to her is the number of years between the birth of a woman and the time in which she, herself, becomes a mother, which in the case of the Aziru is fifteen years.

Her people had found it difficult to adapt to the world of Zanthodon, due to the absence of cattle. They had tried to domesticate the uld, and a species of deer which roam the far eastern plains, but they had been forced at length to adopt the ways of hunting and agriculture.

By this time, however, her tribe was dying off rapidly. At length, none were left alive save for her aged mother and herself, and a young man her own age named Zuma, the son of the chief. Remaining unmarried until her mother's death, Niema had trekked into these mountains for the mating ritual, for it is the custom of the Aziru for the young women of marriageable age to remove themselves into a place of hiding for a time, while suitors for their hand search for them.

By this time, Niema had hidden in the mountains for several weeks, waiting for Zuma to track her to her lair. Since he had not, as yet, found her, and she was getting heartily sick of waiting for him to come, Niema had decided

to travel back toward the kraal. In other words, she planned
to make it easier for Zuma to find her, she added with a grin.

Niema had concealed her gear behind a rock on discovering she was no longer alone in the hills. Now she led her new
friends to the place where she had concealed her possessions,
and squatted expressionlessly while they examined her
treasure. There was a longbow strung with catgut and a hide
quiver of arrows feathered with plumes from the zomak, a
long dagger of sharp flint which she customarily wore
strapped with thongs to her right thigh, and a blanket roll.

They began traveling together, with Niema generously offering to guide the youngsters toward where they believed
their tribes to be encamped. Her bow brought down a brace
of fat archaeopteryx, which they roasted over a bed of glowing coals, and her two charges devoured the succulent meat
with hungry gusto.

"If Zuma is looking for you to the east, where lies the
town of your people," asked Yualla, "is it not going far out
of your way to accompany us west toward the sea?"

The black warrior woman shrugged carelessly.

"It will not take long, and Niema will not go far," she said.
Then she added, with a mischievous twinkle in her eyes:
"Besides, it will give Zuma more time to yearn for the em-
brace of Niema!"

Yualla laughed and the two women exchanged a glance,
understanding each other perfectly.

They continued west, with Niema striding along in the lead
and the two young people at her heels. She moved with a
gliding, pantherlike grace, and the rolling of her naked hips
and the grace of her long, tapering legs was entrancing to
watch.

Indeed, Jorn the Hunter could hardly keep his eyes off the
black woman. The daylight glistened from her naked body as
if from oiled black satin. He thought her stunningly beautiful,
even breathtaking, in a new and different way from any
woman he had ever before seen. And it did not take Yualla
long to notice his rapt gaze was always fixed upon the bare
buttocks and long legs of the Aziru amazon. Very much a
woman for all her youthful years, Yualla first pouted, then
became piqued. Before long, she left Jorn's side to join
Niema, whom she engaged in conversation as if oblivious to
Jorn's very presence. From time to time, the two women
glanced back at him and giggled.

Jorn flushed scarlet with mortification, and his firm jaw became truculent.

"Women!" he muttered to himself.

They came to a pool in the rocky flanks of the Peaks of Peril, and the two girls decided to bathe. They sternly ordered Jorn to turn his back and stand guard while they divested themselves of their few garments and plunged delightedly into the cool silver shock of the fresh mountain stream which fed the lucent pond.

The two women looked each other over with frank curiosity. The part of the plain of the thantors where the Aziru had built their kraal was very far from the nearest tribal grounds of any of the Cro-Magnon nations, and, while Niema had occasionally seen one of the blond, blue-eyed barbarians from a distance, Yualla was as much a novelty to her as she was to Yualla. She admired the silky softness of Yualla's golden, fluffy hair, and her wide blue eyes, which were very beautiful.

For her part, Yualla found Niema equally interesting. The Cro-Magnons, both men and women, have very little body-hair, but Niema had even less. And her nipples were protruding studs of milk-chocolate brown, different from Yualla's own rosy nipples.

"What is Zuma like?" she asked, as they lolled in the cold embrace of the pool. The black woman sighed.

"He is very beautiful," she said wistfully, "in the ways that men are beautiful. He is as tall as Niema, and no older, a mighty hunter and a brave warrior. It has been long since Niema saw Zuma, and she longs to feed her eyes upon his body. . . ."

"What do you think of my Jorn?" asked the other girl, shyly. Niema grinned.

"He is very handsome." And they went into this fascinating subject in much more intimate detail than I care to record here. Suffice it to say, that Jorn's ears would have burned crimson had he been able to overhear their words.

Chapter 7.

GORAH OF KOR

When Hurok the Apeman disappeared so mysteriously during our sleep period, the first explanation that sprang to my mind was an alarming one. I feared that Hurok thought himself unwelcome among the Cro-Magnons, and that once we had found our way to Thandar he would be lonely and unliked.

I said as much to the warriors of my company as we broke our fast. In their opinion, I was wrong.

"In the opinion of Varak, my chieftain is mistaken," said my Sotharian friend. Parthon and Warza agreed with him, and they quickly told me how Hurok had risen by popular acclaim to the rank of chieftain of my band, when I had lain captive in the Scarlet City. His strength and endurance, his indifference to danger, and his innate wisdom and common sense, had won first their grudging respect, then their admiration, finally their love.

I had been reunited with my friends too briefly to have heard more than a sketchy account of their adventures during my absence. Now this cursory narrative was filled in with further corroborative detail. I was heartily relieved to learn that my huge friend had won the affection and liking of my warriors, but puzzled as to what had impelled him to flee from us, if it was not the fear of finding himself alone and unwelcome.

Ragor the Thandarian shrugged philosophically.

"That we may only know when Hurok tells us, my chieftain," he said, sensibly enough.

"The *real* question, my boy," puffed Professor Potter impatiently, "is: what are we going to *do* about it?"

I looked at my friends thoughtfully.

"My first impulse is to follow the spoor of Hurok through the underbrush, while it is still fresh, and catch up with him if I can," I said. They nodded at each other, grinning.

"The huge fellow will move more slowly than will we smaller and lighter men," remarked Thon of Numitor mis-

chievously, adding, with a sly glance at the gigantic Gundar:
"All of us, save, of course, for Gundar!"

The warrior from Gorad looked at him stolidly, and
grunted as if disdaining to reply to the quip. Gundar is the
biggest man in the twin tribes, this side of Hurok himself, as
I have already explained.

Without further ado, we collected our gear and moved out.
I disliked letting the women go with us, but their mates insist-
ed as loudly as did they.

"I will help as best I can in the finding of Hurok, and
please do not worry about me!" said timid little Jaira stoutly.

"Or me, either, Lord Eric!" added Ialys of Zar.

"There you are, my boy!" said the Professor explosively.
"It is all the 'tribe' or nothing—we are with you, my boy, to
the last man and, ah, um, the last woman, too."

I grinned and accepted the offer, glad that my friends were
willing to join me in the search for the missing Hurok. In the
little time he had been among us, the huge, hairy Neanderthal
warrior had won the admiration of all for his courage and
strength and prowess, and had made many firm and fast
friends.

Without further ado we packed our gear, assembled, and
entered the jungles. I dispatched the fleetest of foot among
us, young Thon of Numitor, to apprise the two Omads of our
brief (we hoped) absence from the twin tribes, together with
our reason for departure. He soon rejoined us, having de-
livered the message.

We moved due west, following the track of Hurok, whose
huge splayed feet had left a trail easy enough to follow. We
knew that we could catch up with the rest of the host without
trouble, since they were journeying south by slow and easy
stages. An army moves no swifter than its weakest member,
and mighty Garth of Sothar was still healing from his wound,
having not quite fully recovered his former strength.

Hurok's motive for leaving us so abruptly was really not so
very mysterious, if you stop to think about it.

In his slow, ponderous way, the huge fellow had been
thinking about what his future life would be like when we
reached Thandar. That he would be the only one of his kind
among us did not really bother him, for he regarded me as
his brother, and had become good friends with many of the
warriors of Thandar and Sothar, and knew that his place in
our councils was as secure as his place in our affections.

No, but he *was* lonely. . . .

When Grond of Gorthak had joined our company with his mate, little Jaira, and when Varak of Sothar had wed Ialys, the slim, dark Zarian girl, the nature of his loneliness had risen to the fore of Hurok's mind.

In a word, he had no mate, and was about to venture far into the southlands, where none of the Drugars of Kor had ever dwelt.

That night, while standing his watch, the great Neanderthal had pondered his predicament. He was aware of our position in the jungle country, and knew that at this point we were nearer to his homeland of Kor than we would ever be again. Indeed, the rocky island of Ganadol lay not far off the coast, amid the waters of the Sogar-Jad, easily reached by dugout canoe. Since so many of the warriors of Kor had been slain in the stampede of the thantors, the shes of his tribe were doubtless by this time lonely and restless, yearning for the companionship of their males. It should not be particularly difficult for Hurok to persuade one of the lonely shes to join him on the journey south.

And he remembered one of the young shes he had known in the cave country of Kor long ago. Her name was Gorah, and she had been too young to mate with a male, although by this time she would be ripe and ready. . . .

So, taking up his flint-bladed spear and his stone war axe, the Apeman moved off into the depths of the jungle as soundlessly as one of his size and tonnage could move. Skirting the encampments of the various Cro-Magnon companies, he circled the area, moving toward the sea.

Exactly how he planned to cross the waters of the underground ocean Hurok did not know. He could not swim, but he could paddle to the island's shore on the back of a log, probably.

When at length he reached the shore, the lumbering Neanderthal prowled up and down the beach, looking for a piece of driftwood large enough to sustain his weight, or a log fallen into the shallows. To his considerable surprise, however, he came upon something he had never expected to find.

Drawn well up under the cover of the bushes, he found a number of dugout canoes fashioned by the hands of his people!

Scratching his sloping, russet-furred brow, as if thereby to somehow stimulate the process of cognition, Hurok puzzled over the mystery. At length it occurred to him that when the hosts of Kor had landed on this beach in order to pursue the Cro-Magnons, they must have come by a fleet of dugout canoes, which they would have dragged up the shore to conceal among the bushes. And, since most if not all of the Apemen had been trampled to death beneath the feet of the thantors, or woolly mammoths, the canoes must still be hidden.

Having solved the mystery to his own satisfaction, Hurok dragged one of the dugouts down into the shallows, clambered aboard, and began plying the crude oars.

The quicker he got to the cave country and found Gorah, the quicker he could persuade her to go with him, and return to rejoin his friends among the panjani, was the way his thinking ran.

For he never had any intention of leaving us for good, had my huge and faithful friend, Hurok of the Stone Age. . . .

We moved through the jungle aisles as swiftly as could be managed, following the tracks of our friend.

At this hour, for some reason, the jungle was silent as a crypt. If any predators were awake and on the hunt for food, you could not have known if from the deathly silence. Which was in itself, now that I think of it, odd. Ordinarily, the jungle is filled with small life, rustling through the bushes, scampering through dry fallen leaves. It is only when the great killers are hunting their prey, that the jungle falls silent—which should have given us a signal.

High on a branch above our heads, a silent figure lurked motionless, only the tip of its long tail twitching in the tension of the chase.

For hours, the great cat had roamed the jungle aisles in quest of meat. But the presence of so huge a host of men in the jungle had scared the small and timid creatures into hiding, and the hunter went hungry.

Our first warning was almost our last, for without the slightest sound or warning, the great cat sprang among us, leaping from its bough to crouch, snarling, baring dripping fangs as long as daggers, momentarily confused by so many prey to choose from.

It was a vandar—the monstrous ferocious sabertooth tiger of Ice Age Europe—one of the most fearsome killers that ever stalked the earth!

Hurok drove his clumsy canoe through the waves of the Sogar-Jad with all the iron strength of his mightily muscled arms. The vessel was a crude one, a mere hollowed log, and it negotiated the underground sea with difficulty. But at length, driven by his tireless thews, it beached upon the rock-strewn shores of Ganadol.

He dragged the dugout up the shore and concealed it as best he could among the tumbled boulders. Then he looked about him with a certain nostalgia he would have been the first to gruffly deny. But it had been long since last he had visited his island home, and he sniffed the dank salt air gratefully.

Prowling among the rocks, Hurok scaled a slope and began to make his way to the narrow valley that was the country of Kor. There many caves cleft the sheer walls of stone, and in those the Apemen of Kor made their homes. Not certain of his welcome after so long an absence, Hurok decided to approach the cave country with circumspection.

Rounding a bend, he came abruptly upon a dramatic scene. Cowering against a rock there lay a woman of Kor; her fur garments had been ripped from her body and bending over her in menacing posture was a huge, hairy Korian male, a stone club clenched in one huge fist and raised threateningly. It was easy for Hurok to read the lust that flamed in the little red eyes of the male as he lowered above the helpless she, and to know that in another instant the male would hurl himself upon the she and crush her feeble resistance before the fury of his passion.

Without even pausing to think, Hurok unlimbered his heavy stone axe and sprang from behind the boulder, thundering forth his challenge.

The huge male whirled upon him, inflamed eyes blazing with rage. An instant later, the two males crashed together, swaying in savage combat, locked in the crushing embrace of each other's powerful, apelike arms, while the female watched wide-eyed in horror—

"Bending over her in menacing posture was a huge, hairy Korian male."

Chapter 8.

STRANGER FROM THE TREES

When the giant sabertooth landed in our midst, we instinctively bolted in all directions. Warza dropped spear and shield and sprang up, seizing a branch, swinging himself up into the treetops. The Professor jumped, squeaked in dismay, and flung himself into the gap between two trees. The others scattered in every direction, and this was from prudence, not from cowardice. In the tiny glade there was no arm room for us to fight the vandar. And, anyway, as it was twice the size of the largest Bengal tiger ever seen, it was wiser to take to our heels than try to fight the monster.

As for myself, I dived headlong into the wall of head-high bushes directly in front of me. Landing, scratched and bruised, on the far side, I found myself at the top of a decline, lost my balance, and rolled down to the bottom, where a small stream gurgled between wet stones.

Leaping to my feet again, I plunged into the nearest jungle aisle. Moments later, hearing no pursuit, I paused to catch my breath. Looking around, I discovered with a sinking sensation located somewhere about the pit of my stomach, that in my hurried flight, I had lost all sense of direction. I could not at once remember from which avenue I had come, or how to return to the little glade later, hoping to rejoin my company.

Cursing myself for a damned fool for panicking so blindly, I looked around, studying the foliage, and eventually decided to travel in one direction. It seemed to be the right one.

I moved through the brush cautiously, knowing I had not had time to come very far from where we had sundered ways. I could have called out, for surely my friends were not far away, but hesitated to do so. I had no particular desire to attract the attention of the hungry vandar, should the brute still be in the vicinity, which I hoped it wasn't.

The jungle was deathly still again, which meant the hunter was aprowl. . . .

By this time I had unlimbered the .45 automatic I carried slung at my waist in its homemade holster of reptile hide, together with the few precious rounds of ammunition which still remained. These were carefully wrapped in oiled leather against the damp. The automatic was clenched in my fist, ready for instant use, should the huge cat make its reappearance.

I went through the jungle for a time, finding nothing. It is a peculiar thing about jungles, which I have also found to be true of forests, and that is: when you are in the middle of one, one part of it looks identical with every other part, which is why even seasoned backpackers find it so fearfully easy to get lost in the woods.

It would have helped if I had a compass with me, but I had none, and the peoples of Zanthodon are still too low on the scale of technology to have developed such a useful instrument.*

In place of the compass, the savage tribes of Zanthodon have, over the ages since their remote ancestors first took refuge in the Underground World, developed a natural sense of direction, which they possess to an uncanny degree. This does not seem to be true of the more recent arrivals in Zanthodon, however, for I have never noticed the talent displayed by any of the Barbary Pirates or by the inhabitants of the Scarlet City of Zar.

Not being native to Zanthodon, my own directional instincts is vestigial, at best. . . .

I had no way of knowing that, all the while, a pair of sharp eyes were scrutinizing my every move. These belonged to a man who lay stretched out on a high branch of one of the taller trees, a Jurassic conifer. He was nearly naked, save for his sandals, a bit of hide twisted about his loins, and his weapons and accouterments. With narrowed, thoughtful eyes, he watched me as I blundered back and forth beneath his high place of vigil, trying to find the proper direction in which I should go to rejoin my comrades.

As he reached a decision, his fingers closed about the shaft of a bow. With swift, silent movements, he nocked the bow and set a flint-bladed arrow in place, held at the ready.

---

* In fact, since the cavern-world lies many miles beneath the earth's crust, I am not altogether certain that a magnetic compass would have worked in Zanthodon.

I had no warning of what was about to happen. Grumbling and cursing under my breath, I plowed through stubbornly intertwined bushes, flailing away at the leafy branches which stingingly whipped my face, my sandaled feet sinking in rotting leaf mold and rancid mud.

Emerging from the underbrush, I found myself in a grassy glade of some size which I had not seen before. And I knew I was traveling in the wrong direction, for I had not come this way, even in my hasty flight from the fangs of the sabertooth.

I was about to turn on my heel and strike out at random in another direction, when leaves rustled overhead.

In the next instant, the magnificent figure of a nearly naked black man swung from the branches above to land lightly as a cat on the emerald turf.

His bow was bent, the arrow nocked and ready. Before I could think or move or speak, he loosed the deadly shaft directly for my heart!

Shivering miserably, Murg huddled beneath a bush in the drenching downpour, as uncomfortable as a wet cat. Against the trunk of the tree opposite from where he crouched whimpering and whining to himself, Xask sat stoically enduring the discomforture of the shower. The two had fled across the plain to a tall stand of trees wherein they had thought to conceal themselves from the huge, hairy omodon who had slaughtered Xask's guards. As things turned out, of course, their precipitous flight had proven unnecessary, as the great cave-bear had lingered behind to assuage its appetite on the corpses of the Zarian warriors.

But, of course, the two fugitives had enjoyed no prescient forewarnings of that; so here they squatted, wet and miserable, and winded from their race across the plain.

When the brief downpour ended, gray clouds drifted away across the dim golden skies of Zanthodon, Xask rose purposefully, kicked Murg to his feet, and led the way back across the vast meadowlands in the direction in which they had made their futile flight.

The vizier kept up a steady pace that was almost a trot, and as for poor little Murg, he must scamper along at the same pace or be left behind.

Xask was in a hurry to rejoin the Zarian legion, for he had thrown away his weapons and stripped off most of his gaudy armor in order to lighten himself for the serious job of running away from the omodon. And he was by now experienced sufficiently in the wild ways of the Underground World, to know that a man without arms or guards or comrades survives but briefly in this land of perils.

He had a comrade in Murg, of course, but the sniveling and cowardly little man was too feeble and too fearful to be of any use in a fight.

By this time, Xask wisely knew, the legion of Zarian warriors had either conquered or been defeated. At any rate, the battlefield would be or should be littered with discarded weaponry and with the arms of the slain. There might, even in defeat, be a few of the warriors of Zar lurking in the vicinity over whom he could exert his authority.

Xask had one main purpose in life, and that was to preserve in one piece the tender and precious hide of Xask. After that, all other plans and schemes and motives were purely secondary. . . .

Without pausing to rest, the two made their rapid way back to the open space at the mouth of the pass before the Peaks of Peril where the three-way conflict had taken place. Here Xask was discouraged to find no survivors of that conflict who had remained in the area. However, he did find a quantity of weapons, from which he selected a thrusting trident and a long, leaf-bladed knife; these he tucked into his girdle.

The thodars on which the mounted officers of the legion had ridden here had long since wandered off, so the two were forced to go forward on foot. They trudged through the pass and headed for the edges of the jungle. After a while, Murg looked inquiringly at his silent companion.

"Whither do we go, master?" he whined ingratiatingly.

The vizier indicated the trampled grasses, which marked the passage of many feet.

"In the direction the savages traveled," replied Xask. "I still have hopes of recovering the thunder-weapon, and of learning the secret of its manufacture." He did not bother explaining further.

Murg chewed this over in silence. Then:

"How do you know we are following the host of Thandar?" he asked timidly, fearful of incurring the wrath of his companion, whose intellectual machinations were beyond the grasp of Murg's furtive little mind.

"The weapons we found discarded were of Zarian workmanship, and of the strange, swarthy men who appeared from nowhere," said Xask crisply. "So were the corpses.

Therefore, the savages of your tribe triumphed over my own
people and either took them captive, or slaughtered them, or
drove them away."

Murg thought about that for a while. He admired the per-
ceptiveness of Xask, whom he regarded as possessing intelligence vastly superior to his own, in which he was, of course,
quite right.

"Then why—" he began, but Xask cut him off abruptly.

"Save your breath," he snapped, "for running."

"Um," grunted Murg, subsiding.

It took Xask and Murg what must have seemed like an in-
terminable length of time to cross the plains and return to the
scene of the battle. For, despite the urgency which drove him
on, Xask could not, after all, travel at any faster pace than
whimpering little Murg would maintain, otherwise he would
have had to leave the pitiful fellow behind. And Murg could
develop a pebble in his sandal, a limp, a stitch in his side, or
a thorn in his foot—anything to slow the pace to what was to
Xask a maddening crawl—with the greatest of ease.

They paused to make a scanty meal, and to sleep. And
they had to pause to rest and drink, for Murg could get thirst-
ier more often than seemed humanly possible, and shortness
of breath was among his many failings. In all, it seemed to
take them forever to get back to the battlefield.

It is really not so difficult to understand why Xask kept the
miserable Murg with him, useless encumbrance that he was,
rather than slitting his throat and going on alone.

Xask was one of those people who cannot feel superior
without having a distinctly inferior person around, so as to
shine by comparison. Also, it pleasured him to have someone
to cow, to bully, to intimidate. Earlier in these adventures,
you may recall, he had similarly bound the hapless Fumio to
his service.

At any rate, so long as he had the likes of Murg to kick
around—verbally, rather than physically—Xask was happy
enough.

What made him even happier, shortly thereafter, was the
two people he found curled sleepily together amid the long
grasses, sound asleep.

It was the very two he most wanted to find, Jorn the
Hunter and Yualla of Sothar!

Cautioning Murg to silence with a curt gesture, Xask unlimbered his trident and crept forward to hold at bay and

disarm the two, before they could once again elude his clutches.

Then he felt the spearpoint between his shoulders, gently pressing in—

Chapter 9

HUROK FINDS A MATE

Niema slept but briefly, and rose to find the two Cro-Magnon youngsters fast asleep in each other's arms, with Yualla's golden head pillowed on the youth's shoulder. A tender smile softened the austere features of the black woman. Only a few years their senior, she felt vastly more mature than her charges, and had developed a genuinely maternal affection for them both—in particular for Yualla, whose spirit she admired.

They had traveled for hours, tracing the line of the range, and arrived at the southern end of the pass through the Peaks of Peril, only to find that the tribes had passed this way into the south. Weary from the long trek, they had paused to refresh themselves and to eat, then felt slumber stealing upon them.

Leaving the two to their cozy dreams, Niema took up her weapons and set forth to scare up some breakfast. She ranged across the grassy plains, running lightly and swiftly, her long bare legs flashing, as she tested the air with sensitive nostrils. She had tasted her fill of roasted zomak and now she hungered for the juicy taste of succulent uld.

In time she found a waterhole, concealed herself in the bushes and crouched there immobile for a considerable length of time. Her patience was eventually rewarded when her bow brought down two fat, quivering eohippi, which she gutted, washing the meat clean in the gushing stream which fed the waterhole, and, slinging her kill across her strong shoulders, returned to where she had left the sleeping youngsters.

Niema's expertise at hunting was only equaled by her skills in warfare. The Aziru, in her time, were a dwindling people, and the women of the tribe fought at the side of their men, and were often as fierce and implacable as Amazons. Whether this had been the case when the Aziru had lived in the Upper World, I have no idea, but it was certainly the case now. She could fight and hunt as well as Zuma, for al-

56

though her bodily strength was less than his, she was swifter on her feet, more agile, and a better runner, being lighter of build.

But I digress.

Approaching the place where she had left Jorn the Hunter and Yualla of Sothar safely asleep, Niema was startled to observe two strangers advancing upon them stealthily. The black woman flung herself prone in the grass, and wriggled forward on her belly as lithely as any serpent, until she had come up to the scene.

Then, as the one whom she would later know as Xask approached with drawn steel while the other, a shriveled and cowardly looking little man with skinny legs and fearful eyes, held back timidly, she waited until his back was turned, then came to her feet in a supple movement and set the hard, sharp point of her assegai between his shoulder blades.

Xask uttered a choked cry, paled to the lips, and turned to give a wide-eyed glance over his shoulder. At the sight of the magnificent naked black woman, his eyes widened all the more. Never having seen a member of the Negroid race, he was paralyzed with astonishment. This may explain the fact that he did not move a muscle, although that spearpoint between his shoulder blades may have had something to do with it.

"My . . . dear young woman," he protested faintly. But, at the grim expression in Niema's lovely face, he permitted the words to ebb away into silence.

His voice roused Jorn and Yualla from their sleep. They sprang up with a gasp, snatching at their weapons, but there was no need for their assistance, as the black amazon had the matter firmly under control.

She looked at the Cro-Magnon boy. "Do you know this little man?" she demanded. "When I approached, he was creeping up on you with that funny-looking spear in his hand. Shall I kill him for you now?"

Xask gave voice to a bleating cry that was meant to be a suave, light laugh.

"My dear boy, please explain to this . . . remarkable young woman that we are old and valued friends!" he said hurriedly, casting a placating smile in Jorn's direction. "Finding you and your little friend alone and undefended, I was merely coming to your assistance when this—this—"

Words failed him—which very seldom happened to Xask.

With a grin, Jorn quickly explained to Niema that this was

the man from whom they had recently escaped, and who had been obviously pursuing them all this while. He disarmed the vizier while Yualla strolled over to where Murg squatted, snuffling and trembling, and searched him for weapons.

Niema grinned, remembering Xask's smooth words, which reminded her of one of the wise proverbs of her people, which she repeated to Jorn.

"The serpent has a pleasant voice, but he carries poison in his mouth," she said succinctly. Xask flushed and tried to look indignant.

Jorn bound his wrists and ankles with thongs, then retired a short distance away to discuss the matter with the Aziru woman. Now that Xask was helpless, what were they to do with him?

"If we just let him and Murg go, they will sneak after us again, hoping to catch us off guard," said Yualla. Jorn nodded seriously.

"And yet, if we have to take them with us, we'll have to keep an eye on them every moment!" he explained.

They explored the few avenues of action open to them without coming to any conclusion that sounded satisfactory. It was Niema who came up with the most practical solution to the problem.

"Let me put my spear into him," she suggested. "The other little man can do us no harm, but *this* one is sharp and clever. He will work us ill, if he can figure out a way to do it."

Jorn was mightily tempted. The Cro-Magnon tribes have a rude code of justice which our effete civilization might consider overly swift and sanguinary. Still and all, it went against Jorn's grain to just spear a bound man, even an enemy, in cold blood and leave him to rot.

In the end, they decided to take Xask along with them. And without further ado, they started off in the direction of the jungle's edge, following the trail of trampled grasses which was clearly the route the twin tribes had taken, a spoor so blatantly obvious that even city dwellers like you and me would have had no trouble in following it.

Of course, they took little Murg along with them. So insignificant and harmless did the sniveling little wretch seem that Niema had ignored him when springing to hold Xask at bay, and they had not even bothered to bind him.

No one ever paid much attention to Murg, and it was hard to believe him capable of causing any harm—an oversight which at least one of the small party would have good and grievous cause to regret later on.

Her heart pounding against her ribs, Gorah of Kor watched with wide and fearful eyes as the two Apemen battled for her. The male who would have raped her was one Ugor, a feared and hated bully whom all of the shes despised. Hurok she recognized at once, although she had not seen him for many months, and, in common with the rest of the folk of Kor, believed him long since slain.

Ugor might have been a bully, but he was a magnificent specimen of Neanderthal manhood, nearly seven and a half feet tall and tipping the scales at four hundred fifty pounds of solid beef. Hurok was a few inches shorter and several pounds lighter, but his fury more than made up the difference, for he had instantly recognized the cavewoman as she he had come to Kor hoping to find.

As their blood heated in the frenzy of combat, and the red haze of murder-lust thickened before their eyes, the two Apemen forgot their weapons and grappled hand to hand, breast to breast, gorillalike arms locked about each other, straining every thew and sinew in the effort to break the other's back.

Gorah of Kor would not have seemed attractive to you or me, for the Neanderthal women are hardly less heavy, hairy and huge than are the males of their species; but everything that was feminine in her thrilled her to the core of her primitive heart as the two males fought for possession of her body.

The mating rituals of the Apemen of Kor were rude and simple. Any male may bellow his claim to any female of marriageable age who is not already mated, and then he must fight to the death any male who challenges that claim. So the outcome of the struggle was a matter of vital interest to Gorah, since the result would decide her future life. And she would have vastly preferred Hurok for her mate rather than Ugor.

The battle was noisy and ferocious. Hurok broke Ugor's grip by ramming his elbow into his adversary's throat. Ugor grunted, gagged, and let loose. Then he kicked Hurok in the belly, and when he fell to the ground, sprang upon him and began trying to break his ribs with vicious kicks of his enormous splayed feet.

Hurok kicked him in the groin, and Ugor sagged to his knees, spewing up the contents of his belly. Hurok hit him in the side of the head with one huge fist—a blow that would probably have crushed the skull of an ox. Ugor fell over backwards, then climbed stiffly to his feet and tried to brain Hurok with a rock he had picked up.

Hurok moved his head to one side so that the blow whistled past by a fraction of an inch, and hit Ugor full in the face, smashing his nose to gory ruin. Ugor blinked, shook his head dazedly, then lowered his head and butted Hurok in the belly. Hurok caught Ugor in his arms and they fell over backwards, blunt tusklike teeth snapping as each tried to tear out the other's throat.

The Apemen of Kor have yet to learn the Marquis of Queensbury's pugilistic niceties, you will observe.

Eventually, Hurok doubled up his legs, planted both feet in the middle of Ugor's chest, and kicked him ten feet away. He slammed up against a boulder and sagged there, dazed and groggy. Hurok staggered over, caught his adversary with a firm grip on both ears, and bashed his head against the rock. He got a punch in the belly in return. Shrugging it off, he slammed Ugor's head against the rock several more times until at length he managed to crack the other's skull.

Letting go of the limp corpse as soon as he was reasonably certain that it *was* a corpse, he let it fall to the ground and lurch over to where Gorah crouched, her small eyes filled with awed admiration. He caught her by the arm and pulled her to her feet.

"Hurok came back to Kor to find a mate," he said thickly, between mashed lips. "Of all the shes, Hurok desires most that Gorah become his mate."

It wasn't much of a proposal, I suppose, but it thrilled Gorah to the heart. She smiled timidly.

"Hurok has fought Ugor for Gorah, and Hurok has won Gorah for his mate," she said quietly. Hurok looked down at her.

"It is what Gorah would desire?" he asked. She looked surprised and faintly scandalized at the question, but nodded happily. The huge male put his great arms around her and held her against his hairy breast. She nestled there contentedly. Hurok was covered with blood and had just sustained a beating that would have killed you or me in the first exchange of buffets, but in the eyes of Gorah he was wonderfully handsome.

He hugged her, wincing just a little at the pain it caused one or two cracked ribs. But then he hugged her again because the pressure of her body against his own felt very good to Hurok.

"Hurok comes hither in a dugout which he concealed in the rocks," he grunted. "Hurok wishes to leave at once to rejoin his friends, the panjani. Gorah must go with him now."

Gorah did not understand what the Apeman her mate could possibly mean by referring to the panjani as his friends, for there is eternal warfare between Drugar and panjani and it has been so since the world began, as far as she knew. But she did not question her mate on this topic.

Together, they made their way through the tumbled rocks down to the beach, where Hurok had concealed the dugout.

Approaching within view, Hurok froze, a warning growl rising in his deep chest, gesturing the female to silence.

Five armed Drugars had found the boat, and were examining it curiously.

Chapter 10.

ZUMA SAVES A LIFE

The man who had dropped from the trees to land lightly before me on the sward was the most magnificent black man I had ever seen. Nearly naked, his splendid body was black as ebony, and glistened with an oiled sheen in the shafts of daylight that speared down through the leafage overhead.

He was several inches taller than six feet, with broad shoulders, a lean waist, narrow hips, and long rangy legs. His hair was a cap of tightly curled black wool, fitted closely to the contours of his skull. He had a long neck, strongly handsome features, and long hands. A double necklace of the fangs of the sabertooth was clasped about his throat; crudely hammered copper wire was coiled about his left wrist; a leathern quiver of arrows was slung across his back and a long flint knife slept in its fur sheath, which was strapped to his upper thigh.

I absorbed these details in one, all-encompassing, lightning-swift glance. Most of my attention was on the arrow pointed (it seemed) at my chest. He drew back the bow and released it and it flashed over my right shoulder to thud into some obstruction behind me and by me unseen.

I heard a squall of pain and turned to see the vandar behind me. The shaft the black warrior had loosed had sunk to the feather in its eye, piercing the brain. As I watched, numb with amazement, it writhed, ripping at the turf with unsheathed claws, and died.

I turned to regard the man who had saved my life, which I had not even known to be threatened. Arms folded upon his breast with simple dignity, he regarded me solemnly.

I thanked him in dazed words I do not now recall. He nodded majestically.

"From the branch above, Zuma observed the vandar creep from the cover of bushes, and he knew that the white man was unaware of his danger," the black said in a deep voice. I tried to express my gratitude.

What Zuma—that seemed to be his name—had done was inexplicable. In Zanthodon, each tribe regards the other with suspicion, and regards them as enemies until they are proven friends. This did not seem to be true, however, of the Aziru.

I queried him on the point, and Zuma shook his head slightly, white teeth flashing in a grin.

"My people, the Aziru, have never feared other tribes," he said quietly. "And it would gall the heart of Zuma to have stood idly by and let the white stranger be slain without lifting a hand to defend himself. Zuma would feel less than a man had he not helped a stranger in need."

I told him that my name was Eric Carstairs, and asked of him his story. We had been conversing in the universal tongue of Zanthodon, which he spoke well enough, though with a slightly foreign pronunciation; in later conversation, I noticed that he frequently employed native African words in lieu of their Zanthodonian equivalents. Listening to his story (the same account I have already given through the lips of Niema, and will not repeat here), I realized that his tribe must have been the most recent of all the many migrations of men and beasts into the Underground World. Probably, among themselves, the Aziru spoke Aziri; but they were acquainted with Zanthodonian, as well.

Suddenly, a skinny little scarecrow of a man with white goatee and pince-nez glasses clipped onto the bridge of his nose, with a huge, battered sun helmet teetering atop his baldish head, burst from the bushes and shrank back with a gasp from the corpse of the sabertooth stretched at his very feet. It was, of course, my old friend, Professor Potter.

"Doc, we have a new friend!" I cried cheerfully, introducing him to Zuma. It would have been hard to tell which of them found the other a more remarkable sight, although both were polite about it. While the Professor excitedly queried Zuma, first in Bantu, then in High Zulu, finally in "kitchen Swahili," before discovering that he could speak Zanthodonian, I called my other wandering boys home with a toot at the aurochs-horn bugle which hung at my hip. Faint replies came from scattered points in the various directions; in half an hour, we all gathered in the glen and they were soon acquainted with Zuma the Aziru.

No one had been hurt in the encounter with the sabertooth, for everyone had fled into the thick brush with the same alacrity I had demonstrated. They were delighted to find me unharmed, and were amazed at the appearance of the towering black, never having seen or heard of a man with such a color of skin before. I was impressed with Zuma's natural dignity, and asked him why he had come into these parts of Zanthodon, which were far to the west of the kraal of his tribe.

"Zuma has searched far to find the woman he would win for his mate," he explained. "She is called Niema, and she is very beautiful. Not finding her in the east, Zuma has come into the west, knowing that she must be somewhere!"

"Ahem!" coughed the Professor. "My dear fellow, may we assume this young woman is also of the Negroid persuasion?" At Zuma's baffled look of uncomprehension, he added, "That is, is the young woman, well, black of skin, and . . . all that sort of thing?"

"Niema is a woman of Zuma's own people, yes," answered the tall warrior. The Professor shook his head sadly.

"Then none of us have ever encountered her, I fear," he said, to which the rest of my companions agreed. In fact, until meeting Zuma, they had never even heard of a man such as he.

Zanthodon is a large world, half a million square miles or more, and it has a lot of surprises in it, of which the presence of the last Aziru was only the most recent to our experience.

"We must go on, before Hurok gets too far ahead of us," I reminded my people. In a terse aside, I explained to Zuma that we were tracking a missing friend, and hoped to have caught up with him by now, until delayed by the sabertooth.

"Zuma will accompany his new friends in their search for their comrade," he decided. "Perhaps along the way, Zuma will find her whom he seeks, as well."

We headed for the shore.

Kâiradine had been limping along for a mile or two, his fine boots ruined by seawater and crusted with sand, his piratical finery a bedraggled mess. He had begun the day in a foul temper, but since his companion ignored his verbal excesses and vicious looks in her direction, the emotion subsided into a morose and gloomy mood of depression.

Ahead of him up the beach, Zarys strode lithely along on beautiful bare legs. The Zarian woman, wiser in many ways than the Barbary Pirate, had tossed away wig and coronet, unbuckling and discarding greaves and breastplate, as these uncomfortably heavy encumbrances were no longer needed.

It was her firm intention to walk all the way back to Zar, if walk she must.

She had kept few of her garments and ornaments, as few were needed in her present situation. Under her gilt mail, she had worn a loose, short shift of silky stuff, and beautifully worked sandals adorned her small feet. These she kept, of course, as well as the telepathic crystal by which she had formerly controlled her giant saurian mount. As the Redbeard had tossed away her weapons when seizing her, she was unarmed.

She was a remarkably beautiful young woman, as Kâiradine reluctantly was forced to admit to himself. She strode zestfully along, hairless pate lofty, arms swinging at her sides. The brisk wind from the sea molded to the ripe contours of her handsome figure the light silky garment that was her only clothing. From time to time, a mischievous gust flirtatiously lifted the hem of her short skirt, revealing to the eyes of the buccaneer the succulent rondure of her pert buttocks and the tender flesh of her inner thighs.

Kâiradine swore feelingly to himself, mentioning the Sacred Well of Zemzem and the Black Stone of Kaabah in distinctly disrespectful terms. The moody corsair did not know what was wrong with him, and was gloomily baffled by his own behavior. If the beautiful young woman was not, after all, the Darya for whom he so long had lusted, she was enough like her to have been her twin sister, and was certainly no less beautiful or desirable. Why, then, had Kâiradine let her sleep untouched all night, instead of having his will of her?

Kâiradine did not know the answer to that question, and as he clumped along unhappily, he puzzled over it.

She was the most intimidating woman he had ever known, was Zarys of Zar! She had a way of glancing at him with a cool, disdainful look of appraisal and a slight, questioning lifting of one brow that made him seem foolish even to himself. With a frosty smile she could quench his ardor or tie his tongue in sputtering knots.

In her presence, he felt clumsy and ungraceful. As if to prove it, at that very moment, the Redbeard tripped over a piece of driftwood and fell flat on his face in a puddle of water.

Sitting up, dripping and covered with sticky wet sand, he climbed to his feet, only to find that the act wrung a cry of surprised pain from his snarling lips.

Zarys paused to glance back inquiringly over her shoulder at him. When she saw him squatting in the wet sand, trying to take off one soggy boot, she came back to where he sat and elevated one brow questioningly.

"Well . . . ?"

"Turned my ankle," he grunted sourly. "When I fell. Hurts."

She stood watching as he inched down the ruined footgear to probe gingerly at his foot. The injured member was swelling visibly.

"Soak it in the sea," she suggested solicitously. "Maybe it will feel better."

"Go wading in the shallows like a child?" he demanded scornfully, although privately he knew it was a good idea. She shrugged.

"Limp along on it then, and bite back the pain. But keep up with me!"

He tried, but the effort made him gasp.

"I can't," he admitted sullenly. Stripping off the other boot, he waded out into the shallow water until it was above the level of his sprained ankle, and stood there with his pantaloons rolled up and the dripping boots held in his hands, feeling foolish.

Zarys gave an exasperated sigh and sat down on a rock. She looked around, appraisingly.

"Then we must stay here, I suppose," she said. "Well, it looks safe enough; there are no beasts about. Perhaps we will have to sleep here, as you seem to be done with walking for a time."

Kâiradine growled something unintelligible in a thick voice, but evaded her eye. She gave him a bright smile.

"While you're standing there," she advised, "take out that shiny sword of yours. Maybe you can spear a fish or two for dinner!"

The Prince of the Barbary Pirates snarled an oath and threw one of the boots at her, which she evaded easily with a delighted and mischievous laugh.

Somewhere, the gods were smiling.

Of all the women in the world I could *have carried off,* thought Kâiradine Redbeard venomously to himself, *I had to carry off* this *one!*

PART THREE

Perils of Kor

Chapter 11.

THE LEVELED SPEAR

Now that we were together again, we resolved to continue on the trail of Hurok. But first we had a problem to solve. That is, when the sabertooth had dropped down from the trees among us, we had scattered in all directions. By now, gathered in the long glen where Zuma had rescued me from the fangs of the huge cat, we realized that we had forgotten our direction, and since we could not retrace our steps to the last place we had seen the tracks of Hurok, we had no trail to follow.

When we explained the problem to our new friend, Zuma shrugged and grinned, white teeth flashing in his ebony face.

"If the feet of your friend are as huge as you say they are, then it should be easy enough to find his spoor, since you say he is traveling in the direction of the sea. Let us make a line, with as much space between each warrior as possible without losing sight of one another, and head in that direction. One or another of us will find the spoor."

It sounded like a good idea. Actually, we didn't know for sure that Hurok *was* heading for the shores of the Sogar-Jad, but while we had followed his trail, he had certainly been heading in that direction.

Since we had to do something we resolved to try it. Spreading out into a long rank, and trying to keep within sight or, at least, earshot of each other, we advanced through the jungles, studying the ground for signs that Hurok had come this way.

A quarter of an hour later, as nearly as I can judge, a *halloo* came to our ears and we gathered to the spot as quickly as could be managed.

It was timid little Jaira, Grond's sweetheart, who had found the trail! And there it was, as big as life and even larger: the unmistakable imprint of the Apeman's huge, splay-toed feet in a patch of mud beneath a conifer.

"Good work, Jaira!" I smiled. "Those blue eyes are sharp as well as pretty, eh?"

She flushed rosily, smiling with pleasure.

From that point on, we could move more swiftly, and also keep together rather than remaining strung out in a line. Zuma proved to be the ablest tracker of us all, and took the lead. Time after time, his gaze unerringly spotted the signs of Hurok's progress through the underbrush. Even the Cro-Magnon warriors, keen-eyed hunters all, were not as good at it as our new black companion.

I have to confess that I am terrible at tracking a trail. Something about urban life in modern civilization seems to sap and vitiate the keenness of a man's senses, and while I have sharp eyes and all that sort of thing, I was not raised from the cradle in the wild, or trained from boyhood to follow a spoor. So all of my friends, except for the Professor, of course, were very much better at it than I. And of them all, Zuma was the best.

I was already developing a healthy respect and liking for this magnificent specimen of manhood, and I hoped that we could assist him in searching for his sweetheart, the girl Niema, for by this time, of course, he had fully explained the nature of his own quest.

But first we had to catch up with Hurok.

When we got to the seashore, it became easy to follow his steps in the sand. We tracked them to the place where the Drugars of Kor had, long ago, concealed their dugouts, and realized what he had intended.

Zuma pointed.

"See the marks in the sand? They are the same width as the bottoms of these hollowed logs. And they go down to the waterline, as do the prints of his feet. Your friend has taken to the sea!"

We looked out across the heaving expanse of the Sogar-Jad, feeling disconsolate. For now we realized the goal toward which the mighty Neanderthal had been journeying. Not far across the sea lay the island on whose southern tip was situated the cave country of Kor.

Hurok was going home. . . .

The island was not visible at this distance, of course, for the air of the Underground World is steamy and the sea usually has a layer of humid mist floating above its waves. But it was there, all right, we all knew.

"Heh, my boy!" chirped the Professor unhappily, "what do we do now? It appears that our Neanderthal friend has returned to the cave country to rejoin his people. Doubtless, he felt he would be miserable, being the only member of his species in Thandar . . . and we certainly cannot attempt an invasion of Kor! Surely, not all of the males were slaughtered during the battle and the stampede of the woolly mammoths. . . ."

"No, I guess that would be a foolish risk to take," I said unwillingly.

"After all, my chieftain," remarked Varak, "if Hurok our friend wishes to return home, he is free to do so. Varak is only sorry that the Drugar did not pause long enough to say farewell."

"I suppose you're right, Varak," I said moodily. "Sure, Hurok is free to come and go as he chooses. But it's just not like the huge fellow to take off without a word . . . something smells wrong about this, and I can't figure out what!"

We loitered about the beach, unable to think of what to do next. I have to admit, ashamedly, that not one of us even so much as guessed at Hurok's desire to take a mate, before returning to join us on our journey south to Thandar. It simply never occurred to us, I guess.

"My chieftain, shall we hasten to catch up with the tribes? They will be well along the journey by now, and we shall have to hurry." It was Warza who spoke.

"I suppose you're right," I said. "I can't think of anything else to do. . . ."

The Professor laid his hand on my arm.

"Eric, my boy! If Hurok intends to catch up with us later, after his visit to the cave country, surely he will be able to do so. He can follow the tracks of the twin tribes as easily as we can. And if he had no intention of rejoining us, but has simply gone back home, then that is the way things are . . . pray do not worry yourself needlessly!"

I nodded, and gave a brief order.

We turned about and entered the edges of the jungle again, heading south after the tribes.

Hackles abristle, Hurok crouched behind a great rock, his new mate whimpering fearfully behind him. He peered around the side to observe the huge Neanderthals as they prowled about his dugout canoe. The males sniffed at the boat, growling guttural remarks to one another.

"What shall we do, O Hurok?" whispered Gorah. Her mate did not know what to say; had there been only two or even three warriors about the boat, he might have risked all by challenging them, and, if it came to a fight, might conceivably have won. But they were too numerous and too well armed, for besides heavy stone axes, they bore throwing-spears and flint knives held to their sides by thongs.

And Hurok had only his spear and axe.

"We will wait and see," he grunted. Gorah subsided, willing to leave such decisions to her mate.

She recognized two of the Apemen at the boat, and identified them to Hurok.

"The leader is Borga, the chieftain, a mighty fighter, the killer of many warriors," she said in muted tones. "His friend is Druth, the Fat One, who terrorizes the shes. He is a great coward and bully, and the shes he chooses to bother with his attention are the very young and timid ones. When she was younger, he used to follow Gorah about and try to catch her when she was alone. . . ."

Hurok growled, indicative of understanding, and a red light flashed in his eye. Still, he held his peace and hid from the warriors. All he wanted was to return to the mainland with the female who had agreed to companion him in life. The last thing he wanted was a fight, not here and now. He was bruised and battered, lame and limping, after his tussle with Ugor, and knew that he would not be at his fighting best until later, when he had rested and dressed his wounds.

Something was happening down below. Hurok peered around the side of the rock, straining his ears to make out the grunts and mutters of speech.

The huge male whom Gorah had identified as Borga had given commands to one of the other males, who now went up the slope and vanished among the rocks, heading in the direction of the canyon which was the center of the cave community. Hurok guessed that Borga had dispatched the male to warn the Korians of the secret arrival on their shores of an unknown party. While the others remained behind to watch by the boat for the return of the strangers, in order to frustrate their escape from the island, the warrior would alert the community of danger, and would probably return with reinforcements, and even a search party to comb the tumbled rocks for the hiding place of the invaders.

Hurok crouched on his hunkers, and he was stymied. He could neither escape to sea with Gorah, since the boat was under guard, nor hope singlehandedly to fight off all the males of Kor. If he remained in hiding here, the searchers would discover him and he would have to fight. But where else could they go?

He turned, touching Gorah, and led the way off through the rocks. The center of the island was a mass of cliffs, honeycombed with caves and passageways, but the base of those cliffs, fringing the shores, was a maze of broken rocks in which a thousand men could hide.

With Gorah following closely at his heels, Hurok prowled through the winding ways. He did not exactly know where he was going, but it was his intention to find a place where the two of them could hole up until such time as they could return and find the boat unguarded, or steal another.

He rounded a corner, and almost ran full into a giant Neanderthal, who growled, bristled, lifted a stone-bladed spear, and leveled it against Hurok's hairy breast.

Chapter 12

KÂIRADINE KILLS!

The tribes of Thandar and Sothar had moved through the jungles on their way south for many hours. At length they came to a break in the maze of trees, and found a broad and grassy plain before them. Not far to the east, the plain was bordered by a tall, conical mountain, about whose crest a plume of inky smoke floated, obviously an active volcano, of which the Underground World had many to boast.

Garth, by now largely recovered from the dastardly attack of the assassin, Raphad, and Tharn of Thandar, met at the forefront of their people to confer.

"That is the Mountain-That-Smokes," said Tharn. "Fire Mountain, we call it. By it, we know our route for certain. This country is new to you, I know, my brother; but we know it well, for by that sign and other landmarks, we traced our way into the north in search of the Drugar slavers who carried off my daughter, the gomad Darya, and Fumio, and Jorn, and others."

"Herein you and your scouts must be our guides," replied Garth. "For, even as you say, none of the Sotharians have ever ventured into these southerly parts of Zanthodon," and with those words, the High Chief of Sothar broke off and stiffened. Tharn turned to follow his gaze.

A ways beyond where they stood at the jungle's edge, the plain turned into a boggy, swamplike morass. Floating mists hovered above mossy hillocks which thrust above the stagnant, muddy waters, and trees grew sparse and twisted.

Amid the veils of foggy vapor, humped, enormous shapes moved slowly—a dozen, two dozen, thirty of the moving mountains of flesh.

"Grymps!" said Tharn in a terse voice.

And they were indeed grymps, or a species of dinosaur which our science calls triceratops. Armored in tough, almost bulletproof hide, the huge saurians, which resembled rhinoceroses more than anything, but were as big as Mack trucks and must have tipped the scales at ten tons each, were among the most fearsome and dangerous and virtually unkillable of the predators of Zanthodon.

"Have they sensed our presence?" asked Garth in low tones.

"I am not sure," answered Tharn. "But one thing is certain: until the herd has moved on, we dare not challenge them by crossing the open place. . . ."

Even as they conversed, one huge bull, obviously on guard, sniffed the odor of man-flesh on the humid air. He raised his great beaked snout, armed with the thick, heavy horn, and bellowed a warning. The cows and the young squealed and gathered into a group, while other males trotted out to join the sentry, the earth trembling under their ponderous tread.

Behind the two chiefs, the hundreds of warriors had left the jungles and stood on the exposed plain near the edge of the swamp. The bulls trotted back and forth, tasting the air and raising their snouts to roar their challenge noisily. Their small eyes were too weak to clearly discern the humans, but their noses were keen enough to make up for the lack of eyesight.

There were very many men near, they sensed. And, in their experience, the presence of so many warriors meant that they were hunting. And it was the first duty of the bulls to defend the herd, which was largely made up of females and their young, against such a band of hunters.

"We are in for it, I fear," grunted Garth somberly. "Before we can get our people back into the relative safety of the jungle, they will charge."

"I fear that you are right, my brother," growled Tharn. And even as he spoke, the first bull burst into a thunderous charge. Head lowered, massive nose-horn pointed in their direction, the huge reptile hurtled toward them at startling speed, followed by six or seven more of the younger, feistier bulls.

Tharn grasped his spear and leveled it, but even as he did so he knew the gesture was a futile one, because you cannot kill or even wound grymps with a spear, and the monster, huge as a moving hill of armored flesh, would be upon them before they could turn to flee.

They did, after all, feast on fish, although Zarys was the one who caught most of them, for the saber-thrusts of Kâiradine Redbeard proved largely ineffective. But he scooped a hole in the sand, packed it with dry driftwood and grasses, touched it to fire with the flint-and-steel in his pouch, and on the glowing coals that resulted, they roasted the succulent finny feast and dined heartily. Not long thereafter, weary from the day's exertions, they sought their rest.

The place they found themselves in was a cozy nest, backed by a tall stand of Jurassic conifers, with thick bushes to afford shelter against the warm, drenching rains, and watered by a small stream of fresh water which came meandering across the plain, to empty at length into the Sogar-Jad.

As usual, they slept well apart, each curled up beneath their own bush, and Kâiradine kept his sword close to hand, lest they be surprised in the sleeping-period by one of the predators that roamed this world. His ankle was less painful by now, for immersion in the warm waters of the sea had helped soothe the bruised and aching muscles, and the Barbary prince had stayed off the injured limb for hours.

After an hour or two of slumber, the quiet was suddenly riven asunder by a thunderous, shrieking cry. Kâiradine snapped wide awake and sprang to his feet, ignoring the pain that stabbed through his ankle. He snatched up his saber and stared about him.

Through the bushes came a fearsome sight. It was the size of a small automobile, and covered with shaggy long fur of reddish tint. Its huge, heavy head, was crowned with an immense spread of horns, like those of some super-bull. Which is precisely what it was—an aurochs, a prehistoric ancestor of the buffalo and the bison.

Sighting the man, it lowered its head, tore at the turf with one hoofed foot, then, gathering its strength, hunching its heavy shoulders, it burst into a thunderous charge and came down upon the lone man like an avalanche of living flesh.

Kâiradine Redbeard sprang out into the open, so as to divert the charging beast from the place where the young woman crouched in fear beneath her bush. The huge aurochs swerved, to charge down upon him.

For a long, breathless moment, the Pirate Prince stood as if taunting the enraged bull with his presence, waiting to make certain that the beast's charge was wide of the place where the woman was sheltered. And, as the great aurochs hurtled upon him, Zarys of Zar clenched both hands against her bosom, as if to still the tumult of her beating heart. Never had she seen such desperate courage, such rash foolhardiness, as the man she had humbled and humiliated, mocked and laughed at, risked life and limb to draw the charging aurochs from her.

At the last possible moment, the swarthy buccaneer sprang to one side—but not quite soon enough, for the sharp tip of one of the huge horns raked his forearm, ripping the flimsy material of his blouse. Blood spurted crimson in the daylight and Zarys flinched to see it.

Kâiradine stumbled, thrown off-balance by the impact of the blow, but, swift as a striking cobra, he thrust out his sword. Like a bull fighter in one of the arenas of Spain, he sank his blade to the hilt between the eyes of the giant aurochs, transfixing its brain.

It was a lucky stroke, a chance stroke, but he struck true and good. The bull hurtled past where Kâiradine stood staggering. It tore the blade from his grip as it thundered on. Then it halted, stumbled, fell to its knees, rolled over on one side, kicked feebly a time or two, coughed a gout of scarlet blood.

And died.

In the aching silence that followed this noisy, tumultuous scene, the Zarian woman released the breath she had been holding in a long sigh of tremulous relief. She was pale as milk; now, under the stare of his dark eyes, she flushed crimson like a faint-hearted virgin.

No words were spoken.

And then the Barbary Pirate limped over to the enormous corpse and slowly and laboriously drew his sword from its skull. He felt numb all over, and shaken, but a feeling of masculine triumph welled up within him. He turned to the woman, who by now had risen to her feet and who stood staring at him wide-eyed. In truth, his feat seemed almost miraculous, for the prehistoric buffalo weighed tons and the blade of Kâiradine Redbeard was no more than a slender saber, easily snapped in twain.

Their eyes locked.

He limped toward her, the blood-soaked sword dangling from his hand. They exchanged no words. He thrust the sword in the grassy turf, bent, caught her by the shoulders and flung her prone on the ground. Then he bestraddled her, and with strong hands ripped asunder the flimsy garment she wore. Her naked breasts thrust free of their imprisonment, and her slim legs parted as he ripped and tore the cloth.

He clasped her roughly in his arms, hot lips searing her face and bosom with fiery impetuous kisses, as he claimed her, as he took her. Nor did Zarys struggle, but lay limp and unresisting in the grasp of his powerful arms, while emotions hitherto unknown raged through her heart and shook her to the roots of her soul.

Zarys had known many men, as Empress and as woman. She had taken love hungrily and given herself casually, despising the soft, effete courtiers who had shared her life for an hour, a night, a week. But never had she known a man like unto the Redbeard: fierce, passionate, ungentle, even brutal in his lovemaking, a man who took rather than gave, a man whose tireless virility left her drained, shaken, exhausted, yet more deeply and richly fulfilled and satisfied than had any other man before him.

They rested naked in each other's arms, panting, dewed with sweat, breathing heavily. Drowsily, he drew her to him and she flowed against him unresistingly, letting him drink slow, deep kisses from her luscious mouth.

He fell asleep with his head pillowed on her flawless breasts. But Zarys lay awake a long time, holding her man, stroking tenderly with the tips of her fingers the hair that drew at his temples, staring dreamily up at the sky, and thinking her own secret thoughts.

After a time, she, too, slept. And dreamed restful, happy dreams. . . .

Chapter 13

WHEN THE WORLD SHOOK

When Hurok and Gorah turned the corner and came so unexpectedly upon the Apeman, Hurok growled and bristled, hefting his heavy stone axe as the Neanderthal thrust his spear toward his breast. Without difficulty, Hurok batted the spear aside and swung his weapon to crunch into the hairy side of his adversary.

Blood spurted; ribs snapped. With a surprised grunt the huge male went down, but there were three more in single file behind him. As Hurok sprang to engage the second, Gorah saw the third male lift a heavy rock and swing it high to bash her mate's brains out.

She dodged, snatched up the spear the first Apeman had let fall, and drove it into the throat of the male who held high the heavy stone. He went down with a crash, and the fourth turned and fled hastily, believing the two to be only the advance guard of a larger number, since they fought with such ferocity and recklessness.

By this time, Hurok's mighty axe had cloven in the skull of his second foe, and the brief but furious battle was over and done. Hurok growled and bristled, gazing around for more males to kill. Seeing none, he turned to inquire after Gorah and to see if she had been injured in the tussle. To his surprise and gratification, he saw her plant her heel against the breast of the male she had slain, in order to pull free the spear she had picked up.

"Gorah is not hurt," she replied breathlessly, in answer to her mate's question.

"Hurok is proud of Gorah, that she fought by his side and did not flee in fright as many females would have done," grunted the Apeman. "And he is proud of Gorah, that she has killed in the defense of her mate."

They embraced briefly. Then, adding to their store of weapons from those that had belonged to the slain, they continued to make their way through the jumble of fallen rocks

"He saw her plant her heel against the breast of the man she had slain and pull free the spear."

and massive boulders. Although Hurok was alert and wary to the possibility, they did not encounter any further opposition. Erelong, they found themselves in a part of the island which Hurok vaguely remembered from days gone by, when he had been a chieftain of the cave kingdom.

He peered, blinking nearsightedly, down at the scene. It was a sloping beach of hard gray sand strewn with rocks, washed by the shallow tides of the Sogar-Jad. Nudging Gorah, who crouched at his side, he inquired in guttural tones:

"Is this not the place-of-boats? Hurok seems to recall it from former memory."

The female indicated that it was. This, then, was the place where the Korians had launched their brief, ill-timed, disastrous attempt at an invasion of the mainland, which attempt had ended so gruesomely under the thundering feet of the stampeding thantors. Few, if any, of the Apemen had returned to Kor alive and unharmed from that fiasco, in which Uruk, High Chief of Kor, had himself fallen. But there might still be a few dugouts on the shore. Hurok discussed this with Gorah, and she reluctantly agreed it was worth a try.

"If Hurok and Gorah can find a dugout here, and not have to return to where Hurok left his own craft, then they can evade the neccessity of doing battle with those who guard Hurok's boat farther down the shoreline," he grunted.

With great care, he prowled through the rocks, seeing no sign of any guards posted here to protect the dugouts—for, after all, why would any be needed to guard them?

In the mouth of a low cave, high up the slant of shore, he indeed found to his delighted satisfaction a number of dugouts drawn under cover to protect them from the elements. Summoning his mate to his side with a low call, Hurok dragged the best of the dugout canoes down to the waterline, held it steady while Gorah clambered in, shoved off, and dragged himself in beside her.

Both plied the crude oars, maneuvering the clumsy boat into the current.

Before long they saw, with relief, the craggy silhouette of the island fade in the misty haze behind them, and naught but the open waters of the sea before their prow.

Even encumbered by their prisoners, Niema the Aziru and her young friends, Jorn the Hunter and Yualla of Sothar, made good time crossing the plain. Once they were within the jungles, of course, their pace was slowed by many obstructions. With the magnificent black woman taking the lead, they moved through the dense thickets of underbrush, wove a path between the boles of mighty trees, and found at length a jungle aisle that seemed to lead in the direction they wished.

Here and there, they found the unmistakable tracks of the tribes all going in the same direction. Niema probably did not intend to accompany her young charges all the way to a meeting with the Thandarians and the Sotharians, but to see them far enough along their journey so as to be assured of their safety. In her heart, the amazon desired to meet at last the young warrior, Zuma, whom she knew to be still searching for her. But she had developed a fondness for the Cro-Magnon youngsters, being a warmhearted and impulsive young woman, and knew that, for the moment, they needed her more than Zuma did. For the two youngsters to have kept watch over the wily Xask and woeful little Murg would have been flirting with danger, and the Aziru woman firmly resolved to see them safely along their journey.

They could travel no faster, however, than little Murg would travel, and the limbs of Murg were thin and crooked and easily wearied. He was forever tripping over roots, falling down, or becoming entangled in vines or thorn bushes. He got out of breath as often as he got a thorn in his foot or a pebble in his sandal, and that was *quite* often.

Niema quickly became exasperated with the whimpering, wheezing, limping, complaining little fellow. She longed to take him behind a tree and put her long knife into him, if only to put him out of his misery. Jorn, of course, was too squeamish to permit her this liberty, if only because he intended to bring Murg before Garth of Sothar for judgment for his crime in attempting to ravish Yualla while she slept, if for nothing else.

Privately, Niema thought that Jorn was a bit too noble of heart for his own good, but she kept this opinion to herself. And smiled understandingly, whenever he said something of this nature, to see the adoring expression in the melting gaze Yualla turned upon her young gallant.

Niema was all woman, and understood the hearts of her sisters under the skin. Still, she thought Murg an unneccessary burden and wished something would come along to eat him up.

As for Xask all this while, the former vizier of Zar was maintaining his silence, making himself as ingratiting and as unobtrusive as possible. He kept an expression of genial, affable, friendly cooperation as best he could, and never once got in the way, made difficulties, or tried to escape.

But all the time, his clever, ingenious brain was at work, striving to think of a way out of this predicament. While Xask greatly doubted that Eric Carstairs or the others would go so far as to have him executed, he did not wish to spend the rest of his days as a slave in Thandar. Not when he could escape and return to a life of ease, importance and influence back in the Scarlet City of Zar—or whatever of it was still standing after its god Zorgazor, the gigantic tyrannosaurus, had gone on his mad rampage. . . .

Without appearing to do so, he took every opportunity to overhear the conversation between his three captors, and to watch and study their every move. The youth and his jungle sweetheart were obviously madly in love: they walked along the jungle trail holding hands, murmuring endearments in low tones to each other, paying little heed to anything else. It was safe enough for Xask to dismiss them from his mind, for they were a million miles away, and would not have noticed whether he and Murg were in the vicinity or not.

Niema was something else, an unknown factor in his wily calculations. He tried to draw her out with seemingly innocent questions, but she replied in short, brusque terms and his attempts at conversation soon lapsed. The beautiful black woman intrigued, fascinated, even mystified the vizier, for her presence indicated the existence of an unknown race in Zanthodon which he had hitherto never encountered.

Since she or the Cro-Magnon youngsters made no reference to how she had come to be with them, or even mentioned Zuma, she remained a mystery to Xask. But that her woodcraft and wariness were of the first order, he was quick to note. She and she alone was the one whose vigilance he must elude.

But even Niema must, at times, sleep. And it was for that Xask waited patiently—that or some unforeseeable interruption which might afford him the opportunity to escape from his captors.

His moment came even quicker than Xask could have hoped.

One moment they were striding alone, single-filed, through the jungle aisle, with Niema at the front, Xask and Murg in the middle, and Jorn and Yualla in the rear, when it happened.

The whiff of sulphur visited their nostrils, cutting through the rank odors of jungle flowers, rotting leaves, rancid mud.

The the earth jumped under their feet.

As a horse quivers her hide to dislodge an annoying fly, the ground trembled underfoot. Was it an earthquake, or the ponderous, stalking tread of some mighty predator?

Jorn gasped; Yualla cried out in fear; Murg screeched—

The earth shuddered violently underfoot! Noise roared in their ears, as trees came crashing down, tearing through brush and clinging branches, to thump against the shivering earth.

Niema stood, arms akimbo, legs wide, feet braced against the violence of the quake.

A Jurassic conifer broke in half, and toppled toward her.

Jorn yelped and sprang to pull the frozen girl aside.

And Xask whipped about and plunged into the thick brush, with Murg at his very heels.

Chapter 14.

FIRE MOUNTAIN SPEAKS

When Kâiradine Redbeard and Zarys of Zar awoke, it was to find the whole world changed about them.

To put it simply, they were in love.

The Empress of Zar had never known a man like Kâiradine and could hardly have dreamed that such a man existed. For the men of her race were either oily-tongued, self-seeking courtiers, ready to flatter and lie and bribe to achieve their ends, or cruel, clever men of greed and ambition. The Prince of the Barbary Pirates, in contrast to the men she had known, was a bold and swaggering buccaneer, accustomed to taking by force that which he desired, and holding it by the strength and skill of his sword arm and the daring and cunning of his mind.

Zarys had never been taken by force before, and found she rather liked it. The smooth, diminutive, effete lovers she had known she had felt contempt for; now, at last, she met a strong man rather like herself . . . but even stronger.

All that was woman within her—and Zarys was quite a lot of woman—gloried in that fact.

As for Kâiradine, he had known complaisant slave women and docile harem girls before, but the pride and courage and fierce independence of Darya of Thandar had totally captivated him. And here was a woman even more proud and courageous and filled with an even fiercer sense of independence, who so closely resembled Darya that he had for a time mistaken the one for the other.

Their lovemaking the night before had been wild and furious, he had been tireless and rough while she had been insatiable, matching him lust for lust. It had been a night of passion such as neither had ever experienced before, or could ever forget.

What, then, was to be the future direction of their lives together? For apart neither of them ever wished to be again.

After the first meal of the day, they discussed the situation

85

honestly, each telling the other of their station in life, and describing the way of life they were each accustomed to.

"Let us make our way back across the plains and through the mountains to the Scarlet City, my beloved," Zarys urged. "You will find my city in ruins, but a strong man of will and decision such as you are will take command and soon put things to rights again! We shall rule side by side thereafter, for I will share the throne of Zar with you, and I will bear you lusty sons and healthy daughters to carry on our line into the unknown future."

The Redbeard was strongly tempted, but he had his own kingdom to consider.

"Let us return instead to El-Cazar, my beloved," he suggested. "There we will rebuild my corsair fleet, and rule over a lawless realm of piracy and loot and rapine, and I will lay at your feet the plunder of many tribes and towns."

His injured ankle by now much less painful, they continued the discussion while journeying into the north along the shore.

When we see them last, dwindling into the distance, they are still talking about it. And here I must shamefacedly confess that I do not know the ending of their tale, for I have no way of knowing whether they returned to the Scarlet City of Zar or to the pirate stronghold of El-Cazar.

Perhaps they visited both; they may even have welded the two realms together into a maritime empire similar to the seagoing ancient Crete from which Zar had sprung.

I do not know. But they had found each other, and were in love, and never troubled Zanthodon again, or at least, not the part of it that I am familiar with. . . .

So farewell to the jealous and imperious Zarys of Zar, and to the ferocious and lusty descendant of Khair ud-Din of Algiers! The gods who rule our fates devised a cunning and fitting punishment for these two magnificent villains—

They got married.

When the males guarding the browsing herd of grymps broke into a thunderous charge and headed straight for the tribes of Thandar and Sothar, who had by now fully emerged from the jungles, neither Garth of Sothar nor Tharn of Thandar had an easy solution to their problem.

The two Cro-Magnon chiefs had both faced grymps before, while hunting on the wide plains of their homelands, and knew the monstrous triceratops for a fearful opponent. Armored in their tough and leathery hide, the heavy brutes were all but unkillable: neither spear nor arrow nor sling missile could pierce those hides, and the skulls of the grymps, armored beneath thick shields of horny bone, were unreachable by any weapon known to their armory.

Indeed, the only time I have known a grymp to be killed, in my own experience while wandering through the jungles and swamps of Zanthodon, was when one had the Professor and me treed, and was attacked by a mammoth which outweighed it by a half a dozen tons or more. The thantor broke the back of the triceratops, and if Garth or Tharn could possibly have conjured up a thantor out of empty air at that moment, probably they would have done so. But no thantors were in evidence; there is never a woolly mammoth around when you really need one, it seems!

The two chiefs uttered quick words of command. While the woman and children, the aged and injured of the two tribes sought refuge behind the close-set trees which stood at the fringes of the jungle country, the warriors sprang forward, with leveled spears, whose butts they wedged into the earth so that their points were aimed at the charging bulls.

It was a flimsy sort of defense, but the best that could be managed, under the circumstances.

One of the older, more experienced scouts stood near the place where the two chiefs had taken their stand. He was a man named Komad of Thandar, the best scout I had ever known, not including Zuma and Aziru.

"Like all beasts of the swamp or the plain, my Omads," said the older man quietly, "the grymp fears fire. Mayhap we can ignite the meadow grass and drive them away from our position in that manner."

Garth squatted gingerly, one hand nursing his nearly healed wound, the other hand testing the grass. He raised wet fingers into view, needing no words to tell that a recent rain had dampened the turf beyond any chance of setting it afire.

"They are almost upon us," growled Tharn, briefly glad that his daughter Darya had agreed to take refuge in the woods with the other noncombatants. "Stand ready, my warriors!"

But there was no need, as things turned out.

I have already mentioned the Fire Mountain, as the tribes called it, which stood not far off to the eastern end of the swampy plain.

Even in that same moment as the furious bull grymps

came thundering down upon the line of Cro-Magnon warriors, who knelt with flimsy spears leveled in a futile attempt at defense—the earth *jumped*.

A ball of whirling crimson fire exploded from the black-lipped crater atop the active volcano.

It disintegrated into a shower of crimson sparks and a thick plume of inky, sulphurous smoke.

"The bulls could not stop in time and hurtled over the brink."

Another jet of fire roared from the mountain peak as from the fiery throat of a furnace. The sky darkened with thickening haze of drifting smoke. Sparks fell like burning hail.

The earth cracked open.

As rivulets of blazing molten lava trickled down the stony slopes of the sides of Fire Mountain, a black crack zig-zagged down the slope and across the plain, accompanied by a subterranean noise, a growling and grumbling as if the Earth Giants were stirring wrathfully in their age-old slumbers.

The stampeding bull triceratops veered off nervously as the ground trembled violently underfoot. The black mouth of a yawning chasm opened before them. Hissing clouds of live steam and whirling dust geysered forth in their very snouts.

The crevice shuddered, its edges crumbling. Then the earth groaned again, and the opening widened. The foremost of the bulls could not stop in time and hurtled, squealing like steam whistles over the brink, to fall into the unknown depths.

Tharn steadied himself as the ground bucked and quivered violently underfoot. Trees tore up their roots and toppled slowly to thump the earth. Zomaks fled the treetops, squawking raucously.

The sky darkened under veils of inky smoke. The smell of brimstone was heavy on the air.

The mountain shuddered and belched fire again. A weird rain of hot ash and burning embers floated down upon the plain.

The bulls halted at the edge of the crevasse, snorting and blowing nervously. Soon they heard the squealing of their calves, the frightened lowing of the cows, and turned around to trot back to rejoin the main body of the herd. In time, they moved off across the plain, putting as much distance as they could between their females and young and the burning mountain.

Garth and Thandar looked at each other and grinned in relief.

Then they turned to regard the black opening in the earth. It traversed the entire length of the plain like a great moat. From lip to crumbling lip it was thirty feet across in places, but nowhere in the range of their vision was it less than half that width.

There was no way to cross it.

Which meant there was no way for them to continue their journey into the south.

Riven by earthquakes is the Underground World, where

the ground shudders to the convulsions of hidden volcanic fires and the skies are often black with the smoke of fountaining lava.

Zanthodon, in this instance, had protected its tribes of blond savages from the beasts of the plain.

But it had also marooned them very many leagues from their homeland.

And there was nothing they could do about it.

Chapter 15

FANGS OF DOOM

With strong and steady strokes, Hurok and Apeman and his mate, Gorah of Kor, plied the crude wooden paddles that propelled their dugout canoe across the misty waters of the underground sea of Sogar-Jad.

Behind them, the mountainous island of Ganadol was gradually lost in the fogs that mantled the surface of the subterranean ocean. Neither was sorry to see the rocky isle fade from vision astern. To Hurok, the isle of the cave country teemed with enemies; to Gorah, it held few friends. And, while the savage Neanderthal maiden viewed her future life among the panjani with fear and trepidation, she relied upon the wisdom and the strength of her mighty mate, and was more than willing to let the future take care of itself.

The straits which separated the rocky shores of the island from the mainland of Zanthodon were not wide, neither were they lashed by storms or heavy waves, but they were the hunting grounds of many of the fearsome monsters of the deep. For this reason, then, the two Neanderthals rowed with all the strength they could command, to lessen the time they must spend exposed to the elements.

From time to time, Hurok cast a searching glance behind him. He did not really fear that any pursuit would be attempted, for he knew that the Apemen were lurking about the boat which he had beached upon the southern shores of the island, waiting for him to return. It would be a certain space of time before the bodies of the males he and Gorah had slain would be found, and even longer before it would be discovered that one of the dugouts was missing from the place-of-boats. By then, he knew, Hurok and his mate would have safely arrived upon the mainland and would be well beyond the vengeance of Kor.

A stifled shriek from Gorah roused the Apeman from his reverie.

He growled, bristled, swerved his gaze forward to where

his mate crouched shivering. Her fear-frozen stare was fixed on the steamy waters to one side of the boat.

The waves boiled—parted—revealing the long beaklike snout of a marine monster. Hurok flinched and glared: a huge, jag-toothed spine rose above the waves, clove the floating veils of mist, then submerged again with scarce a ripple to show that it had ever been. But Hurok knew he had not dreamed the sight.

At a glance, he knew the creature for an aurogh, although it had been long ago in his youth that he had last seen one. In a flash, the memory returned to him: a fishing fleet upon the Sogar-Jad, when he and other Drugar cubs were being taught the skills of the sea by grizzled oldster. The scaly monster had overturned the boats, snapping up squealing cubs . . . it was a memory of such horror to Hurok, that even now he swore and flinched therefrom.

As well he might. From the description, Professor Potter identified the aurogh as none other than a monster saurian of the prehistoric seas called the ichthyosaur. Save for its long, beaklike snout, the ichthyosaur resembled a super-shark, forty feet from snout to tail, and every inch of that forty feet crammed with mindless hunger and ferocity. One of the most deadly predators of the ancient oceans was the aurogh, and from the Triassic to the early Cretaceous, it was monarch of the waves.

Thank God, only here in the prehistoric seas of Zanthodon the Underground World did such a maritime monstrosity still live and flourish. . . .

"Is it gone?" whispered Gorah, shuddering. Hurok shrugged.

"I do not know," he growled briefly. "Grab your oar—and row!"

They rowed, crouched low above the gunnels of the dugout, putting all of the strength of their heavily muscled backs and shoulders into the effort. Ahead of them, across a stretch of foggy waters, the dim line that marked the shores of the mainland was vaguely visible—so near, and yet so far, as the saying goes.

Fixing their gaze upon that tantalizingly near line of tree-fringed darkness, the two Korians bent their backs.

It was not enough.

Suddenly, a vast force stirred beneath them. Briefly, the waters boiled to foam about the craft. Then it lifted suddenly into the air—and was flung afar!

The ichthyosaur had arisen a second time from the deeps of the Sogar-Jad—directly beneath the keel of their dugout—and had flung the craft into the air as a rising whale might do, coming up for air under a whaling boat.

Hurok was thrown clear, the paddle flying from his hand. He whirled like an ungainly bird through the foggy air, and came down to smash into the surface of the underground ocean with shocking impact. It was what we used to call a belly-whopper, and the impact when he struck the water's surface was more than enough to knock the air out of him.

Gasping for breath, with wide eyes he saw the foaming waters close over his head as he sank like a stone, kicking and struggling. Warm water seeped past clenched jaws and stubbornly shut lips, to choke and burn his throat. Floundering with massive arms, kicking violently, Hurok rose to the surface again. As his head broke the waves, he flung back wet hair from reddened eyes and gulped air into starved lungs.

Nowhere could he spy Gorah, his mate.

Hurok gulped air and let himself sink beneath the waves again, reaching out with long arms to clutch and grasp.

He could not swim, could Hurok.

And neither could Gorah, his mate. . . .

We moved through the jungle, my comrades and I, following the tracks left by the twin tribes. We knew that they were not, could not be, very far ahead of us, and that very soon we would catch up with the rear guard of the host.

We conversed but little, busied with our thoughts. That we would never see Hurok again seemed likely, and those of us who knew him, and who valued the friendship of that mighty warrior, were naturally saddened thereby. So there was nothing to be gained by talking about his absence.

If he had returned to Kor, it could only be because homesickness had overcome him, and the need for the companionship of his kind, a need which all of our comradeship and friendliness could never assuage.

"Cheer up, my boy!" chirped the Professor, toiling along at my side. "Our huge and hairy friend may yet return to join us farther along the journey, and, at any rate, even if he remains in the cave country of Kor, perhaps he will be happier among his fellow Neanderthals. . . ."

"I know, I know, Doc," I grumbled. "It's just that—that,

well, I miss him already. —At least, he could have hung around long enough to say good-bye!"

"And to have given you enough time to talk him out of it, eh?" he said, shrewdly. I winced; I suppose that was what was lurking in the back of my mind.

He patted me on the shoulder, and his lips parted to make some further observation, but just then—

The earthquake struck!

When the ground leaped and shivered underfoot, knocking us asprawl amid the bushes, something like thunder growled and boomed in the distance, and the stench of sulphur and brimstone smoked upon the air.

I staggered to my feet and stared around wildly. Underfoot, the ground quivered like a live thing. Bushes rustled, beasts yowled, trees were toppling slowly to every side, uprooted by the earth tremors.

Great Gundar grabbed my arm, pointing.

"The beach! The beach!" he roared above the noise. I gulped and nodded, to indicate comprehension. Trees were falling to thump the earth all around us, and the open shores of the Sogar-Jad, not very far away, were certainly the safest place for us to be, under the circumstances.

We headed for the shore, stumbling along, lurching as the ground shook underfoot. By now, the air was pungent with the smoke of burning rocks and live sparks and cinders were floating down among us.

The Professor lost his footing and fell to the impulse of another tremor. Gundar bent, scooped the old savant up, tossed him across one brawny shoulder, and pelted on through the whipping bushes. I followed, and the others after me.

Moments later, we burst out of the line of trees and thick underbrush which fringed the beach and found ourselves on the sandy shores of the underground ocean once again. Trees had fallen athwart the beach, but we waded out into the shallows and stood, while I counted heads. Thankful, I saw that we had all escaped unharmed from the earthquake.

Gundar helped the Professor down, and the little scientist peered about at the plumes of smoke in the sky from the distant mountain, eyes snapping with eagerness.

"Fascinating, my boy!" he breathed. "Although the mountains of Zanthodon are ancient, there are still many live volcanoes among them; and vulcanism is active. I had presumed as much from the rock formations I have observed along our journeys, but this is the first eruption I have ever witnessed

. . . Great Galileo, but I wish I were close enough to see the volcano!"

"Be glad you aren't, Doc," I said sharply. "Knowing you, you'd be sticking your nose into a bed of hot lava and get it singed off first thing."

He snorted, but subsided. I guess he realized that I was right.

We waited things out. Within the hour, the earth tremors subsided and the stench of brimstone (or whatever it was) faded from the air, and we deemed it safe enough to return to the interior of the jungles.

By then, we were all hungry, and decided to hunt and eat first, before continuing on the trail of the tribes of Sothar and Thandar.

Zuma proceeded farther down the shore, while others of our number unlimbered bows and arrows or hunting spears. The black warrior guessed that many fish would have been washed ashore in the eruption and earthquake, and spotted tidal pools ahead of us, which he wished to investigate.

Instead, he almost ran into an immense, hairy monster who boomed a savage challenge, hefted a heavy stone axe, and came charging down upon him, growling bestial warnings.

PART FOUR

Crossing the Abyss

Chapter 16.

THE PROFESSOR DEPARTS

Xask and Murg plunged headlong into the bushes and the underbrush swallowed them up. The ground shuddered violently underfoot and bushes whipped violently. As the two ducked and staggered between the trees, the gloom of the jungle was made hideous by the squeal of tearing wood, the thunder of toppling trees, the roaring of panicked beasts.

After a time, as the two ran out of breath and paused to catch their second wind, leaning exhaustedly against the tall bole of a towering cycad, it became evident that the earthquake was over and most of the danger seemed to have passed. The ground trembled no more and the burning whiff of sulphur and brimstone had faded from the humid jungle air.

Murg and Xask looked at one another wordlessly, and Xask smiled. They had escaped safely and were again at freedom, and Xask vindictively hoped the black warrior-woman had been crushed to death beneath the falling tree which had felled her.

"Come over here and free my wrists," he snapped. Murg scuttled to where the other crouched and fumbled nearsightedly at the thongs which bound the vizier.

"Alas, Murg has no knife," he wailed.

Xask shrugged irritably. "Untie me with your fingers, then, and be quick about it! Now that the earth has stopped its shaking, our late captors—those of them that have survived—may come looking for us."

Murg tugged and pried at the thongs. "Murg hopes they all are slain," whined the little man.

Xask glared coldly.

"Best for us that they are not," he stated crisply. "For I still have need of them, as hostages for the secret of the thunder-weapon."

Murg did not know what the other man meant, but wisely

held his tongue, poking and pulling at the thongs. After a
moment Xask added, meditatively:

"And if perchance they are dead, well . . . then I must
think of something else. Aren't you done with that yet?"

"Yes, master!" breathed Murg, and Xask pulled free of the
thongs and briskly began rubbing the circulation back into his
hands.

After a brief rest, they started on. As best they could, the
two retraced their steps to approach the place where the
falling tree had given them their chance to make a break for
freedom. Neither Xask nor Murg had any particular talent as
scouts or hunters, so their woodsmanship was minimal; still
and all, before very long they found the place, but Jorn, Niema and Yualla were no longer there.

Xask studied the turf about the fallen tree thoughtfully,
thin lips pursed. "It would seem that even the black woman
survived the earthquake," he mused. "They must all have
continued on the track of their tribes. In that case, they
would have traveled in that direction," he said, pointing.

Snapping a curt command to Murg, the vizier started off in
the direction which the three were most likely to have traveled. Cautioning his little companion to silence, he slunk
through the woods, making all possible speed, but keeping as
quiet as could be managed, to avoid being discovered by
those he was following.

Unarmed as both men were, they felt themselves fortunate
that the earthquake seemed to have driven all of the beasts of
the jungle into their lairs, where, doubtless, they cowered in
safe hiding. Thus the two were not molested during their
tracking of their quarry.

Xask, busied with his own plans and plots, said but little,
save to snap curt commands to his unhappy little companion
from time to time. As for Murg, the poor fellow was morose
and miserable. He seemed always to be finding himself under
the thumb of those wiser or stronger than himself, and he
was getting heartily sick of it. First there had been the dreadful, cruel Gorpaks, then the Neanderthal bully, old One-Eye,
then he had been taken captive by Yualla of Sothar; now, he
was at the beck and call of the Zarian vizier.

Murg wished there was something he could do about this,
but was too timid and cowardly to think of a course of bold
action that would free him from his present yoke.

Had Xask known of the emotions seething in the scrawny

breast of his companion, he would only have smiled cynically.

Nobody ever paid much attention to Murg. . . .

Professor Potter was also restive, but from more elevated motives of intellectual excitement and scientific curiosity than those which stirred in the heart of Murg. He was consumed with a fervent desire to witness the volcanic eruption at first hand, and at length resolved to do so while we lingered on the beach, waiting for the hunters to return with their catch.

Pausing to scribble a brief note to me on a blank page torn from his little black notebook, he took up a dagger and a light spear, and crept into the jungle. And I must confess that it was some time before any of us discovered that he was missing. When it did come to our attention, I found his note pinned with a thorn to my bedroll, and scanned it quickly. The missive read as follows:

> Eric, my dear boy:
> I simply must observe the active volcano at first hand, and have seized the opportunity to do so while our party is busied with hunting, cooking, and eating. I will be very careful, and will return soon enough, so please do not worry about me!
> Your friend,
> Percival P. Potter, Ph.D.

Blurting a curse, I sprang to my feet, then hesitated. Many of our group were still absent, including the black warrior, Zuma, and my friends, Gundar and Thon of Numitor. Varak looked at me quizzically, it having been that warrior who brought to my surprised attention and consternation the fact that the Professor had departed from our company.

"He will get lost, and then get eaten by a dinosaur, if I know the Doc!" I swore. Varak patted me on the shoulder.

"The old man is smarter than you think, Eric Carstairs, and will not be so foolish as to stray into the jungle without blazing a trail so as to be able to find his way back to us," he said. "And, besides, the shaking-of-the-ground has frightened the dangerous beasts into hiding—see how silent the jungle is? He will be all right, Varak feels certain."

"I sure hope you're right," I said grumpily. The truth was, I had become inordinately fond of the scrawny savant by this time, and dreaded losing him. But, surely, the volcano was not very far away, and, anyway, there wasn't much I could do about the Doc's disappearance. I just wish I had kept a closer eye on him, that was all. . . .

Yet another person was getting restless and worried about things, and that was my beloved princess, Darya of Thandar. Before we left the camping area in pursuit of Hurok of Kor, we had dispatched a messenger to the encampment of Tharn the High Chief, informing him of our mission and promising that our absence from the tribes would be as brief as possible. We suggested that they continue on their way and promised that we would follow their trail and catch up with them a bit later.

Darya had been separated from me too long, and we had only very recently been reunited, for her to feel happy at my departure or comfortable over the length of my absence. So, while the twin tribes were momentarily held at bay, helpless to cross the wide chasm which the eruption and earthquake had opened in their path, the Cro-Magnon girl decided to backtrack and find me herself.

Knowing that her father would sternly forbid such an act, she merely took up her weapons and departed from the host in such a manner that her departure went unnoticed. She did, however, mention where she was going and why in a brief exchange of words with one of the warriors at the rear guard of the host, so that her father would not be unduly worried over her disappearance.

Knowing that Eric Carstairs and his company could not be very far to the rear, this warrior, a man named Bugor, permitted her to leave without trouble. He knew the bold and headstrong Princess from her childhood, and had a hearty respect for her woodsmanship and intelligence.

Entering the thick underbrush, Darya moved on light, swift feet down the jungle aisles in the direction from which the two tribes had come. It was her intention to locate the area in which we had all lain encamped during the last sleeping period, then strike out on our trail, for the cavegirl reasoned that she could follow the spoor of Hurok as easily as we could, and in this, of course, she was correct.

The jungle was silent and seemingly uninhabited as she glided through its aisles and glades and thickets. Darya was an experienced huntsman and her senses were as honed and keen as those of any Mohawk brave's, and she was confident that she had naught to fear. The girl had lived all of her young life in such surroundings, and knew that those predators which were large and ferocious enough to be dangerous, make considerable noise in moving through a jungle as thick as this one, and thus advertise their presence far in advance of their arrival. If any such disturbance came to her notice, Darya intended quite simply to climb a tree in order to remove herself from the path of danger.

But there is one dangerous denizen of the prehistoric jungles of Zanthodon that moves as silently as a gliding shadow, and that is the isst, or giant python, which flourished in primal ages and often attained the astounding length of forty-five feet.

Darya froze, therefore, with a startled yelp when without the slightest warning an immense serpentine shape dropped a coil from the boughs directly overhead, to challenge her passage with a hissing cry from fanged jaws that could open to swallow a full-grown man.

And, in the next fraction of a second, a sharp explosion rang out, deafeningly loud in the ominous silence which pervaded the jungle, and three things happened almost simultaneously.

The huge head of the super-python simply flew apart in a gory splatter.

Immense, writhing coils loosened, and the monster serpent dropped limply to the floor of the glade almost at Darya's fear-frozen feet.

And a man, clothed as she had never before seen, stepped from the underbrush with a smoking rifle in his hands.

Chapter 17

THE BRIDGE OF LOGS

When the tall tree toppled slowly toward Niema, the black girl did not hesitate but plunged directly into its path. Jorn yelled and sprang forward. An instant later, the tree crashed to earth directly on the spot where the Azuri maiden had been standing when the earthquake struck.

In the excitement of the moment, neither Jorn nor Yualla—and certainly not Niema—noticed that Xask and Murg had seized this opportunity for escape, and had taken to their heels and vanished into the underbrush.

Jorn clambered over the tree trunk to find the lithe black amazon squatting amid a thick-leaved bush, shaken but unharmed and smiling broadly. The girl had instinctively realized that to leap backward would have been to come up against another tree, and that safety lay only in jumping under the toppling jungle giant.

"Niema is unharmed," she informed the Cro-Magnon youngsters. They squatted beside her, while the earth tremors subsided. Once the brief earthquake was over, they searched for their two captives and found them missing.

No one was particularly sorry to discover this, and least of all Niema. She grinned, white teeth flashing.

"Niema is happy to see their heels," she remarked, employing an Aziru saying whose meaning is more or less identical with "Good riddance!" Her companions were unfamiliar with the phrase, but grasped it readily enough.

"The earth has stopped shaking and that bitter, burning smell is gone from the air," Yualla pointed out. "Let us be on our way before it starts up again." Her companions agreed with her, and without further ado they continued on in the direction they had been following.

Niema strode along zestfully, fully aware that the earthquake would have frightened the more dangerous beasts into hiding in their lairs for the present, and that this reduced the perils they might face and made a more rapid and less cautious pace possible.

Her keen eyes searched the ground for signs of the passage of many human feet. The spoor she tracked would have been obvious even to you or me, and she followed the path made by the twin tribes as easily as if they had been marked with directional signs.

She had, of course, no slightest notion of what was about to happen next. . . .

When the ichthyosaur overturned their dugout canoe, Hurok and Gorah sank beneath the foaming waves of the Sogar-Jad.

As the water closed over his head, Hurok opened his mouth to yell. Promptly swallowing a mouthful of seawater, he fought down his panic, closed his mouth, and kicked violently to the surface. When his head broke water, he reached out desperately with long and powerful, apelike arms. Flailing about, he touched the slick wood of the boat's keel and locked his grasp thereupon, thus managing to keep his head above the waves. When, a moment or two later, Gorah also reached the surface, he helped her to grab ahold of the overturned boat.

The huge aurogh had submerged again, like the super-shark it was, being unable to breathe the air and needing to return to its watery realm frequently. But it was obviously hungry, the ichthyosaur, and it was hunting.

Hurok feared the creature would bite their legs off underwater, but for all his strength, he was unable to clamber up out of the water and sit astride the overturned hollowed log. It simply bobbed under his weight and would not permit itself to be ridden.

Before long, however, the huge marine monster surfaced again, and bore down on them. This time he could see it clearly, the long beaklike snout, the round eyes mad with hunger and bloodlust. His weapons were lost in the sea, all save for the stone axe lashed to his waist; but, needing both hands to cling to the overturned canoe, he could not unlimber his means of defense, even if it had been feasible or even possible for him to employ spear or axe while immersed in seawater up to his chin.

Gorah wailed in fear, and, to tell the truth, Hurok felt his courage quail, for there seemed no way out of this dilemma. Even if he and his mate had been able to swim, which neither could, they were too far from the shores of the mainland of Zanthodon to have even dared attempt to swim to the beach before the hungry aurogh would be upon them with snapping jaws, ripping and tearing their bodies asunder.

Spotting its prey clinging desperately to the hollow log, the maritime monster bore down upon them, the water frothing to either side of its opening jaws like the fan at the prow of a speedboat. Gorah squealed and shut her eyes, momentarily expecting the jaws of doom to close upon her. Hurok growled a hopeless curse and stoically waited for the end—

But it did not come!

Water boiled behind them and there soared into view an incredibly long and sinuous neck, like the foreparts of the Sea Serpent of legend. Atop this supple neck upreared a head with open jaws fearsomely armed with fangs the length of cavalry sabres.

A yith! thought Hurok to himself, with an inward groan.

As if they were not in enough danger from the ichthyosaur, now the dreaded plesiosaurus of the antique Prime had entered into the competition . . . and the prize was the flesh and blood of Hurok and his new mate!

Tharn brooded at the lip of the chasm that had reft in twain the grassy meadows and the swamps. From lip to lip the crevasse must have measured thirty paces or more, and that was too wide for even the limberest boy in the twin tribes to leap, or the most agile of the scouts. And, even were they able to somehow toss a line to the far side of the steam-belching abyss, there were among the tribes women and infants, the aged, the infirm and the injured, who would have found it impossible to bridge the abyss by swinging hand over hand along such a length of line.

Garth, his brother monarch, the Omad or High Chief of the tribe of Sothar, was among those who could not have made so difficult a passage, due to his recent and but newly healed wound. So the jungle monarch conferred with his chieftains as to how best to circumvent this newest obstacle in their journey south.

"We could, my chief," said one of the scouts, "travel east to the slopes of Fire Mountain, where the crack in the earth began, and attempt to go around it, thus taking ourselves quite some distance out of the way, but at least being able to continue on our way."

They discussed this, but it was obvious that the suggested plan offered even more perils than they now faced, for the rivers of live lava which had poured down the slopes of the volcanic mountain had ignited the brush and dry grass in the foothills, and was still burning.

It was Garth himself who thought of an alternative to this hazardous solution. His sharp eyes had noticed a place near the edge of the jungle where tall trees, felled by the quake, had bridged the gap in the earth. He suggested they cross the abyss by these natural bridges, which looked to be secure enough.

"Even the old and those suffering from wounds can go across the gap by inching along the tree trunks," he said. "I, myself, although not yet having recovered my full strength and agility, feel certain that I could negotiate the abyss in that manner, with time."

One of Tharn's senior chieftains spoke up at this point.

"And, to facilitate our passage of the crevasse, my chief," he said, "could not our warriors, armed with axes, fell yet more trees so that more could cross the gap in less time?"

It was, at length, decided that this was the best idea yet brought forth, and without further ado the two Omads gave orders and men began chopping down those of the taller trees which grew the nearest to the edge of the abyss, while the younger and more agile warriors and hunters crossed by means of the trees which the earthquake had felled, and, calling back across the crevasse, reported the trees secure and unlikely to be dislodged under the weight of men.

In this manner, the men and women of the twin tribes began to cross the abyss. By ones and twos at first, then by the dozens, they climbed across by means of the fallen trees and those other trees the woodsmen had felled. Before long, Tharn himself crossed and so did Garth, albeit slowly and gingerly, favoring the wound near his heart.

By now, the combined tribes numbered in the hundreds, and it consumed much time for so huge a host to gain the other side, but at length, save for the rear guard, it was accomplished.

And it was then and then only that Tharn discovered that his daughter had gone back some time before to find Eric Carstairs and his companions, who still had not rejoined the host. And Tharn found himself in a quandary!

"Curse the wench for a foolhardy child!" he growled, his brow black and thunderous. "If she were here now, I'd turn her over my knee and teach her a few lessons."

"Yes, my Omad," agreed the guard to whom the gomad

Darya had given her message to her father, and his tones were quite unhappy.

"Oh, I don't blame you," said Tharn, seeing the expression on the face of his warrior, a trusted and valiant man of the tribe. And then he added a phrase which we might translate as saying, "the saucy minx could charm the birds out of the trees, if she wanted to," or something to that effect.

"Well, my brother, what shall we do?" inquired Garth of Sothar, who had overheard the exchange. "Now that all of our people have crossed the abyss, we can hardly go back . . ."

"I know," grunted Tharn, seething.

"And the gomad's future mate, Eric Carstairs, is not, after all, very far away, surely! Your daughter the gomad will reach his side soon, and he will follow to the brink of the abyss with all his companions and cross even as we did, for the method we used to cross the gap will be obvious. So, shall we stay here and await their coming, or continue on?"

Tharn, arms folded upon his mighty breast, considered the matter.

"We shall go on," he said briefly.

Chapter 18.

DENIZENS OF THE DEEP

Herr Oberlieutenant Manfred, Baron Von Kohler, late of General Erwin Rommel's famed Afrika Korps, had left the camp that "morning" after breakfast in order to scout out the jungles ahead, leaving the two soldiers, Corporal Schmidt and Private Borg, to tend to Oberst* Dostman, whose wounds were suppurating and who was unable to travel at more than a very moderate pace.

The jungle seemed quiet during their morning meal, but the Baron took along a Mauser rifle and a few precious rounds of ammunition just in case. The Germans were on their way to the sea, which they believed to be somewhere nearby and to the west of their present campsite, but because of Colonel Dostman's injuries, taken when they had been attacked by a stegosaurus, they must move by slow and easy stages, and it seemed wise to scout out the terrain in order to avoid rough or dangerous ground.

The Oberlieutenant was a tall, well-built man, with an erect and military bearing. His close-cropped hair, once blond, was now silver-gray, and the years he had spent here in the Underground World of Zanthodon had left lines in his broad brow and had furrowed his lean, clean-shaven cheeks. But his pale blue eyes were sharp and keen as in his youth, and his step was light.

During the long years since they had found their way down into the gigantic cavern-world beneath the trackless sands of the Sahara, Von Kohler had seen his company dwindle and diminish, some of his fellow officers and private soldiers falling prey to accident and illness, but most of them to the fangs of the fantastic prehistoric monsters who lingered on in this lost world, so much alike to that fabled Andean plateau of which he had read in Herr Doyle's excellent ro-

---

* A rank in the German army comparable to that of a Colonel in our own army.

mance in his boyhood back in Munich. And now that his senior commanding officer, Colonel Dostman, seemed unlikely to recover from the battle with the stegosaurus, Von Kohler was all too aware that soon the responsibilities of command would come to rest solely upon his own shoulders. . . .

When the earthquake struck, he was traversing a ravine in which a small stream gurgled over smooth stones. The shock threw him prone, but he recovered himself a moment later, nerves tingling with shock. Scrambling to his feet, he recovered the Mauser he had let fall when thrown to the ground and fell into a fighting crouch, peering around alertly. Fortunately, the quake was a brief one and soon over.

He climbed up out of the ravine, making a mental note of the fact that the steep incline would prove difficult for Schmidt and Borg to negotiate, as they would be encumbered by the crude litter in which the Colonel was to be carried. He must scout out a better way for them to travel than to climb down into the ravine. . . .

A time later, having found a better means of crossing, he was continuing on toward the sea when a dramatic scene caught his attention and arrested his progress.

Directly before him, through a thin screen of bushes, Von Kohler saw a young golden-haired woman in abbreviated hide garments, bearing a long spear and a bronze knife. He knew her at once for one of the Cro-Magnon savages they had seen but avoided heretofore in their passage through the jungle, and he lingered behind his screen of bushes, knowing that where there is one person there are probably many more, and that the savages of Zanthodon generally travel in full tribal strength. The German officer thought it prudent to conceal himself while investigating the situation.

He saw, although she did not, the monstrous python whose heavy coils hung from the bough directly above her head.

An instant later, the girl froze in terror as the giant snake swung its fanged and gaping maw toward her through the leaves.

The German had been raised with all the chivalrous instincts of his class of the old nobility. Without a moment's thought or hesitation he snapped the rifle to his shoulder and blew off the python's head. . . .

Head reared high above the seething waves, the yith gave voice to a deafening challenge, like the steam whistle of a locomotive. In response, the aurogh gave a vicious snap of its sharklike jaws, and submerged. An instant later the sea went mad, exploding in sheets of spray and boiling foam as the two prehistoric sea monsters closed in mortal combat to decide which of them would devour the hapless Hurok and his mate.

"The fearsome jaws of the ichthyosaur closed upon the scaly shoulder of the yith."

The fearsome jaws of the ichthyosaur closed upon the scaly shoulder of the yith, which uttered a thunderous hiss and swerved its snaky head to rip and tear with saber-sharp fangs at the face and snout of its adversary.

The seething foam became streaked with crimson as the marine monsters battled for their prey. Gorah rolled her eyes skyward and shuddered, as much from the terror of the scene as from the chill of the waves.

Hurok strove again to right the boat, but again he failed, for with nothing against which to brace his huge splayed feet, he could gain no purchase on the wet and slippery wood, despite the iron strength of his burly shoulders and arms. In his struggle, however, he flailed out with both legs and the dugout floated away from the scene of combat.

This gave the Apeman an idea, which he conveyed in guttural words to his mate. The two were clinging to the same side of the canoe, now, in unison, both kicked out with their strong legs, propelling the overturned boat slowly through the foamy waters.

Peering hastily back over one furry shoulder, Hurok saw that the plesiosaur had wound its sinuous length about the giant shark-monster, and was ripping at its flesh with those dreadful fangs, and all the while the triple rows of teeth were crunching deeper and deeper into its mailed shoulder.

As they paddled away from the scene of terror, the two monsters, locked in a murderous embrace, sank from sight beneath the bloody waves, and, although the water continued to rage in turbulence for a time, giving evidence of the titanic battle which roared on beneath the sea, neither surfaced again.

Hurok gave a sigh of heartfelt relief. Had the Apemen of Kor any religious instincts, he would doubtless at this juncture have muttered a prayer of gratitude to whatever divinities watched over the warriors of Kor, but his people were too low on the scale of civilization to have developed more than a primitive awe of the spirits of their dead ancestors.

"Keep kicking," he growled to Gorah.

In time they wearied, and, since neither of the marine monsters had made a reappearance, simply rested, clinging to the hull of the overturned dugout canoe, letting the slow and shallow surges of the subterranean sea drift them nearer and nearer to the shore of the mainland of Zanthodon.

At length, Hurok felt solid mud beneath his feet, and from

that point on the two Korians pushed their craft through the surf and dragged it up onto the sandy shore, and sat down wearily, letting the humid warmth of day dry their bodies and resting from their exertions, glad to feel the firm earth under their feet once more.

Hurok privately swore never to venture any nearer to the sea of Sogar-Jad than the beach thereof, for one ducking beneath the waves was enough to last him a lifetime, and few of the warriors of Zanthodon ever for a second time survive the fangs of the mighty monsters of the deep.

"Where are we, O Hurok?" inquired Gorah in faint tones, exhausted from the perils through which she had passed. Hurok looked around and heaved hairy shoulders in a shrug.

"Hurok does not know," he admitted. The simple fact was that one stretch of sandy beach fringed by the edge of the jungle looks very much like any other stretch of sandy beach fringed by the jungle.

But, as the Peaks of Peril were no longer in sight, the Ape-man knew that they had drifted with the current very much farther to the south than he could have wished. His companions and the twin tribes themselves could be many days' march away in either direction by now. . . .

When they were dried and rested and had fully recovered from their dunking in the Sogar-Jad, the two Neanderthals got to their feet and began to explore. The only weapons they had retained from their sea adventures were the flint knife which Gorah carried at her waist and the heavy stone axe slung about Hurok's hips on a tough leathern thong. These weapons were good enough for fighting at close quarters, but Hurok felt more comfortable with a spear's length between him and whatever beast they might encounter. So they lingered in that spot long enough for him to hew down a sapling and trim its twigs and branches away with blows of his axe.

With the sharp blade of Gorah's knife he sharpened one end of the makeshift spear to a point. Then, hefting his new weapon to his shoulder and taking Gorah's hand in his huge paw, he began trudging up the beach, choosing the northerly direction at pure random.

Hurok did not know just what he was looking for—some sign of his missing friends, I suppose—but what he found amazed and alarmed him. He pulled Gorah into the bushes and bade her squat there while he peered nearsightedly at the peculiar individual he spied coming down the beach.

It was a man, but such a man as the Apeman had never seen or heard of, black as ebony from heel to crown.

Roaring his challenge, Hurok sprang from the underbrush and leveled his spear at the breast of Zuma the Aziru—

Chapter 19.

MEN FROM YESTERDAY

The Professor had tramped through the jungle for quite some time now, heading in the direction of the active volcano in the swampy plains of the south. He encountered no dangerous beasts or reptiles along the way, and was feeling quite pleased and satisfied with himself for his mastery of woodsmanship—when suddenly a loud explosion rang out sharply through the silence of the deserted jungle.

"Noble Newton, but if I didn't know better, I could have sworn that was a rifle shot!" exclaimed the old scientist to himself as the echoes of the sound rang and died, smothered in the thick undergrowth between the boles of the trees.

Inquisitive as always, Professor Potter diverged from his path to circle back, hoping to find the source of the sound. As the only firearm which existed here in the Underground World was my own Colt .45 automatic, the Professor was baffled as to what could have made such a noise—for it certainly was not the metallic bark of my pistol being fired.

Emerging from the bushes, he halted suddenly, eyes goggling in amazement as he found himself looking upon a tense, dramatic scene.

Directly in front of him was a grassy glade. In the midst of this open space there stood the supple, half-naked figure of a young golden-haired girl whom the Professor instantly recognized as Darya of Thandar.

At her feet, writhing in slow death spasms, were heaped the thick, glistening coils of the most enormous python the scrawny savant had ever seen. It seemed to be without a head!

Between the Professor and Darya stood a tall, well-built white man, facing the Cro-Magnon girl with a smoking Mauser rifle clenched in his hands.

His back was turned to the Professor, but the old scientist saw with amazement that the man had close-cropped silvergray hair topped with the battered remnants of an officer's cap—an officer's cap such as those worn by the German Army during the Second World War.

The man was completely clothed in garments of faded khaki, very much worn and carefully repaired, but little more than a collection of scrupulously clean rags held together by needle and thread. The desert boots he wore were dilapidated and long unpolished, but scrubbed clean.

Taking a deep breath, the old man stepped forward and put the point of his spear between the shoulder blades of the German, who flinched and tensed all over, but did not move or even turn his head.

Darya blinked incredulously at the sudden appearance out of nowhere of her lover's friend, then smiled.

"I say, my dear, are you hurt at all?" quavered the Professor in a shaky voice. "If this brute has dared to lift a hand against you, I'll—I'll—"

In his excitement, the Professor spoke in English, although he knew quite well that the Princess of Thandar knew only a few words of that language. But the man into whose back the point of his spear was pressing was acquainted with the language, and turned to look with amazement at his attacker.

He saw a scrawny old man in tattered bits of fur, wearing an absurdly large and very dirty sun helmet, with a white goatee and pince-nez glasses perched insecurely on the bridge of his nose.

All three looked at each other in wordless astonishment, while at their feet the giant reptile slowly, slowly, died.

Recovering from her surprise, Darya lifted her own spear and touched the German officer upon the wrist. He knew precisely what she wanted him to do—drop the rifle—but as the weapon was not on safety and had a hair-trigger, he was reluctant to do so. Addressing the old man at his back in only slightly accented and formal English, he said gently:

"With your permission, sir, I will lower my rifle to the ground, as to drop it might cause it to fire." His voice had good timbre, resonant and cultured. The Professor nodded crisply.

"Please do so, and take care!"

The rifle safely laid at his feet, the officer lifted both hands in token of surrender and spoke again.

"If I may introduce myself, sir, I am Oberlieutenant the Baron Manfred Von Kohler, late of the Ninth Attack Group of the Afrika Korps, at your service!" Worn bootheels clicked together as the officer made a slight bow. "I assure you, sir, that I meant no harm at all to the *fraulein;* my weapon was at the ready in case the serpent was not entirely dead."

The Professor came out of the bushes and looked his prisoner over narrowly. The officer was no longer a young man, and had suffered many privations in the jungles of Zanthodon, from the tattered but patched condition of what remained of his uniform, but his keen blue eyes were candid and alert and his voice was steady.

For his own part, Manfred Von Kohler was examining the old scientist with equal interest and curiosity.

"English?" he inquired with a slight smile. The Professor shook his head.

"American—although I have spent much time in England, and, for that, Germany, too—although of course that was after the ... the ..."

The Professor let his words trail away awkwardly into silence.

"You meant to say 'after the war'?" the German said, completing the Professor's remark. And it was not really a question. The Professor looked a trifle unhappy.

"Yes," he said simply. The Baron looked at him for a moment, and then in quiet tones, asked the question.

"My country lost the war." Again, it was not really a question. The Professor nodded, and Manfred Von Kohler drew a long, deep breath.

"So. Thank you for your candor," he said softly. "The ... Russians, I suppose?"

Professor Potter shrugged. "The Russians, yes; and the Americans, and the British, and the Free French. ..."

The German nodded with a touch of sadness in his eyes.

"So," he breathed. "I knew it was a lost cause. To take on the whole of the civilized world was pure madness ... I was only a boy when I entered the Army, but even then I knew it was madness. Still ... all of these years we have spent in this fantastic world under the sands of the Sahara, with never a word of news, one could not help but entertain ... hopes."

The Professor cleared his throat. "I ... um ... I'm sorry," he said. The German shook his head with a polite smile.

"Not at all. If I may presume, you will be wondering what I am doing here."

"As a matter of fact—?"

Hands still raised, the officer gave a brief explanation.

"My group was cut off from the main body during a desert battle," he said quietly. "When our vehicles ran dry of petrol, we attempted to cross the desert afoot. A sandstorm drove us into seeking refuge in a cave. When the blown sand blocked the entrance to the cave, and we thought we should soon suffocate, we discovered that fresh air was coming from the other end of the cave. We followed the tunnel as it sloped down and down into darkness, and in time we found ourselves emerging into this perennial daylight, in a world left over from prehistoric ages in a cavern larger than we could comprehend. Ever since then, we have been trying to find our way back to the surface, but without any success, I fear."

"An amazing story, simply amazing!" breathed the Professor. The German shrugged.

"We have been here ever since," he finished. "It has been . . . many years now."

"It has indeed," agreed the Professor sympathetically, and he refrained from telling just *how* many.

"There are more of you, then?" Potter asked.

"In the beginning, we were three score, although several were wounded in the desert battle," said Von Kohler. "The fantastic world, as you know, has many perils. Some of our numbers we lost to the depredations of the great prehistoric beasts, others to swamps, earthquakes, fever. But four of us remain alive, including myself. There is my superior, Oberst Hugo Dostman, who was very seriously mauled by a stegosaurus and whom we do not expect to live, and two soldiers, Corporal Schmidt and Private Borg, good and loyal men both. We are encamped not very far off; I came ahead to scout the safest path to the sea, and arrived on the scene just in time to assist the *fraulein* in eluding the fangs of the monster serpent."

Professor Potter was busy absorbing this latest of the many surprises Zanthodon's jungles hide, and so was Darya, who was breathlessly hanging on every word. The conversation, by now, had fallen into a crude sort of *lingua franca*, part German, part in English, and part in the universal language of Zanthodon, the conversants picking up a term from one language where they lacked its equivalent in another.

Darya was able to grasp about one word out of every four, but that was enough for her to get the drift of what the two men were talking about. She touched the professor's arm.

"It is true, what the stranger says," she told him. "I did not even see the isst until he shattered its head with his thunder-weapon. Had he refrained from doing so, Darya would by now be dead and eaten—!" She shuddered at the idea.

The Professor nodded thoughtfully.

"Well, then, my dear Baron," he said tentatively, "I believe that we can permit you to lower your arms to your sides, if you wish, although I most earnestly entreat you not to attempt to pick up your rifle. Both the young woman and myself are remarkably proficient in the employment of these crude weapons," he said with a meaningful gesture of the spear he still held at the back of the German officer.

Manfred Von Kohler nodded and said nothing. He had no doubt that the beautiful Cro-Magnon girl could use the spear with great skill, and would not hesitate to do so, were he foolish enough to try for his firearm, but he rather felt inclined to think that the old American scientist overstated, to some degree, his own skill with the weapon.

"Thank you, sir," he said, lowering his arms to his sides.

And they stood for a moment without words.

"Well," said the Professor at last, clearing his throat uncertainly, "and now we must decide—what the devil I am supposed to do with you!"

Chapter 20.

XASK MAKES A DISCOVERY

With Niema, as usual, taking the lead, the three adventurers moved on swift and silent feet through the jungles of Zanthodon. Jorn and Yualla knew they could not be very far behind their tribes, for so huge a host of men, encumbered with women and children, the aged and the injured, can move only as rapidly as the weakest among them.

Thus it came as no particular surprise to them when, of a sudden, Niema froze, motionless, with a quick gesture at the two Cro-Magnon youngsters behind her, commanding silence.

The bushes parted before where she stood, revealing a tall blond-headed young man armed with a long knife at his waist and a bronze-bladed spear held at the ready. Spying the long-legged black woman, he paused momentarily, eyes widening in amazement.

In the next instant, Jorn and Yualla came crashing forward, and all three embraced, laughing with joy while the Aziru girl watched uncomprehendingly.

"Varak—is it really you!" exclaimed Jorn the Hunter with delight. The other hugged him fiercely, tears of happiness agleam in his blue eyes.

"The question should be—Jorn, can it be that you still live?" declared Varak. "We thought you long since dead from that fall you took from the mountain ledge . . . and, unless my eyes are lying, is not the girl at your side Yualla, gomad of the Sotharians?"

"I am Yualla," laughed the girl.

"Your father and mother will be heartily relieved that you still live . . . but were you not carried off by a hunting thakdol*? By what marvel have you both survived? By what incredible luck do you come to be here? And, before my heart bursts with curiosity, do tell me who that amazing black-

---

* The Zanthodonian word for the immense Jurassic winged reptile we know as the pterodactyl.

colored woman is . . . although I suddenly am able to guess her identity."

Interrupting each other, the Cro-Magnon boy and girl related to Varak a brief and somewhat confused account of their adventures while Niema stood with a warm smile lighting her lovely face, affectionately sharing the excitement and joy of these reunited friends. For Varak, of course, had been on the mountain with Hurok and the others of my retinue when they had striven to seek the Professor and me amid the bewildering ways of the Scarlet City, that time we had been held captive by Zarys of Zar.

Varak interrupted this torrent of narrative just long enough to answer a question from Yualla.

"My news will please you," he grinned. "For we are all together again, or soon will be . . . Eric Carstairs and the Professor are with us, and all of our other comrades, although Hurok had strayed from us, I hope but briefly. And, Yualla, your mother and father, and all of your tribe, are not far ahead, for we parted from them only a little time ago in order to search for our huge and hairy friend. Soon we will all be united again, to continue the journey south to Thandar . . . but tell me, Jorn, how it was that you escaped from the little men of Zar?"

The tale was taken up again, and when at length it came to a narration of the most recent of their adventures, and the two youngsters mentioned how they had been found and befriended by Niema, the tall warrior interrupted a second time, to turn a smiling face upon the silent amazon girl. "If you are truly Niema of the Aziru," he said, "and surely there cannot be two such women as you in all the length and breadth of Zanthodon, then I have welcome news for you, lady, which will be pleasant to your ears, I doubt not!"

"What news is that?" inquired Niema, and, as if by foreknowledge of the words the warrior was about to speak, her heart lifted within her breast in a surge of glorious hope.

"The black warrior who would be your mate, Zuma of the Aziru, is among us and we are already friends!" said Varak triumphantly.

The blaze of joy that lit up Niema's face was truly wonderful to see.

"Can it be the truth?" she breathed faintly. "Tell me that he is well and unharmed, and searches for me still!"

"He is—he does—!"

"Where, then, is he at this moment?" she demanded. Varak
pointed toward the sea.

"We split up to hunt for food for our meal," he said. Hefting his spear with a rueful expression on his face, he added:
"I came into the jungle, hoping to find uld, but the shaking-
of-the-earth seems to have scared them all into hiding, for not
yet have I so much as made a single kill! As for Zuma, he
went down the beach, hoping to spear fish in the tidal pools
along the shallows, and for aught I know paces the sands
even now—"

"*Ai-raa!*" shouted Niema in a loud voice filled with exul-
tant joy, startling them all. And, without another word, the
black girl turned and plunged into the brush and vanished
from their view in the direction of the shores of the Sogar-
Jad, eager not to waste another moment before hurling herself into the arms of the stalwart black warrior whom she had
long desired to take as her mate.

When Manfred Von Kohler blew the head off the giant python to save Darya of Thandar from its gaping jaws, the shot
was heard by other ears than those of Professor Percival P.
Potter.

Moving stealthily through the brush on the heels of Niema,
Yualla and Jorn the Hunter, Xask and Murg were keeping
their quarry in sight when the shot rang out, echoing through
the stillness of the wood.

Xask allowed a gasp of surprise to escape his lips, and
sank his fingers into the skinny arm of Murg. An unholy light
flashed in the dark eyes of the Zarian vizier, for he at once
recognized the sound as that made by the thunder-weapon
which Eric Carstairs carried, although on second thought it
seemed to him that it was different in timbre and in loudness.

How this could be eluded his imagination, for, surely, there
could not be two such weapons in the Underground World—
not since the explosion set by the Professor back in the Scarlet City had totally destroyed all of the weapons which his
wiles had coaxed and coerced the scrawny old savant into
making for him and his Empress.

Instantly abandoning the tracking of the Cro-Magnon couple and the tall black warrior woman who had befriended
them, he turned to plunge through the bushes in the direction
from which the shot had come.

With an unerring sense of direction, the vizier led his whining, stumbling little companion to the glade where they ar-

rived in time to be eye-witnesses to the confrontation between Darya of Thandar, Professor Potter, and the unknown stranger in peculiar garments who held a weapon of dark metal such as neither Xask nor Murg had ever looked upon before.

Xask instantly deduced that it was a thunder-weapon of similar power to the small hand weapon which Eric Carstairs carried and which Xask had long coveted, for in trigger and in barrel it resembled the automatic. He could not imagine how two such weapons came to be here in the jungle world of Zanthodon, but he could not deny the evidence of his eyes.

Cautioning his companion to silence, he crouched in the brush and overheard their conversation. Many of the words and terms they employed were unfamiliar to him, but Xask disregarded this fact, since there was nothing he could do to alter it. Agleam with cupidity, his eyes were riveted on the thunder-weapon as Manfred Von Kohler, with the Professor's spear jabbing him between the shoulder blades, bent and gently deposited the deadly thing on the greensward at his feet.

So fixed was his attention on the scene taking place before him in the glade that he did not notice the stealthy approach of another until Murg timorously nudged him in the ribs to apprise him of the fact.

Xask could see that the second stranger was garbed in clothing similar to the first, in hue and design, and that these were also scrupulously clean but worn almost to tatters and carefully patched. He was larger and fuller of face than the first stranger, and was going bald. But none of these details was of any particular interest to the vizier.

What caught his fascinated eye was the fact that the second stranger *also* bore a rifle similar to that which the first had just surrendered, and that a small hand weapon very much like that belonging to Eric Carstairs, was holstered at his hip.

Glee lit the dark eyes of Xask; there were now at least four thunder-weapons in the Underground World, rather than merely one!

Which quadrupled his chances of getting his hands on one, so that the surviving artisans of the Scarlet City could duplicate them and arm the legions of Zar with a weapon of such irresistible might as to conquer the entire world.

PART FIVE

Soldiers from Yesterday

Chapter 21.

HOW NIEMA FOUND ZUMA

When the huge, hairy giant burst growling from the under-brush to jab his crude spear at the naked breast of Zuma, the black warrior instinctively leaped backward and raised his own Aziru assegai in defense. The two circled each other warily while a second apelike creature, obviously female with full bare breasts, cowered fearfully amid the shrubbery.

Zuma had never faced an opponent so large and im-pressively muscled, or at least not a human opponent. Or was the growling creature before him fully human? His broad, sloping shoulders and long apelike arms were matted with russet fur, and his low, jutting brow and prognathous jaw made him resemble a beast as much as a man. Zuma had lived all of his days in Zanthodon and therefore had never seen a gorilla such as dwell in the jungles of the upper world, but he had heard fearsome tales told of such dangerous man-like creatures from the lips of his grandsires, and this was the first thought that rose to his mind.

The hairy Apeman jabbed at Zuma's breast, but the black with swiftness and agility deflected the spear with his own, al-though the strength of his foe's thrust jolted the black to his very heels.

In a contest of sheer muscle, Zuma knew, he stood little chance against so huge an enemy. All he could hope for was that his intelligence and quickness were of an order superior to that of the Apeman.

He aimed a cunning thrust at the hairy beastman's ab-domen, and, as he had hoped, the other lowered his spear to deflect it. In the same instant, his belly-stroke having been a mere feint, Zuma's point flashed for the other's thick throat.

Gorah—for of course it was she—spied the feint in the same moment, and cried out in fear and warning.

"—*Hurok!*"

Zuma managed to turn his thrust awry in the very nick of time. Amazement flashed in his dark eyes and he stood back, half-lowering his assegai.

"Are you truly the one called Hurok?" he asked.

Blinking curiously, his foe lowered his crude spear.

"Hurok is Hurok," he growled. "But how can that name mean aught to one whom the eyes of Hurok has never beheld ere this?"

Zuma grinned. "I am a friend of Eric Carstairs and the white warriors," he explained swiftly. "They have mentioned your name in Zuma's presence and have related of their search for their missing comrade. I am Zuma, a warrior of the Aziru people."

Hurok examined the tall, lithe black warrior narrowly, rather liking what he saw. Slowly he grounded his weapon and a huge smile creased his thick lips.

"If you are a friend of Black Hair, as am I, then it is good that Hurok and Zuma did not slay each other," he said in slow, deep tones.

Zuma grinned and dropped his own weapon.

"Things could not have turned out happier for Zuma," the black declared. "In truth, the strength of Hurok's arms is such that Zuma is relieved there is no need for us to fight one another. Eric Carstairs and his friends will be pleased that Hurok has returned to Zanthodon, for they were bewildered by your disappearance and have traveled hither in search of you."

Hurok dragged the reluctant she female from the bushes and proudly displayed her to the Aziru.

"Hurok returned to the country of Kor to fetch hither a mate from among the shes of his people," he explained. "Is she not a fine she?"

"She is indeed, and Hurok has every reason to be proud," said Zuma, with some prevarication. In all honesty, the Neanderthal woman looked unappetizing to him, and his memory summoned forth the image of the slim and beautiful young woman of whom he nightly dreamed and for whom he had sought so long.

Gorah then tugged at the powerful arm of her mate and pointed timidly back up the shore.

"O Hurok," she said timidly, "behold where another dark-skinned one approaches!"

Zuma turned to see the person to which the Neanderthal woman referred, and froze as if rooted by sorcery to the spot. For a long instant, the dazed warrior believed himself caught up in another of his nightly dreams, for the long-legged, slim and beautiful black woman who came sprinting lightly down the beach to where he stood in converse with the two Korians was none other than his beloved Niema!

Calling her name, he ran to meet her and caught her up in his strong arms. As she was crushed against the stalwart chest of her beloved, held tightly in the embrace of those powerful arms, her cheek against his naked breast, feeling the pounding of his heart, Niema felt bliss such as she had only dreamed of. Zuma covered her beautiful face with fierce, happy kisses and she smiled and lifted her lips to his.

After a time, he held her away from him at arm's length, his face serious, his eyes stern.

"Niema, daughter of Kirah and Junga, virgin of the Aziru, I, Zuma, the son of the chief Waza, claim you for my mate against all the world," he said formally. "Look not henceforth with the eyes of love upon another warrior, and, for his part, Zuma will no longer look with desire upon any other woman."

She smiled, saying nothing. The ceremonial phrase did not require her aquiescence. But then Zuma spoke another query, softly, for no ears to hear but her own.

"Is this what Niema truly wishes in her heart?" he asked.

"Niema could not ask for more than this," she said simply, "unless to pray that the Ancestors permit the loins of Niema to bear many strong sons and healthy daughters sprung from the seed of Zuma of the Aziru."

While the two Neanderthals watched with only dim comprehension, the two briefly embraced, exchanged a chaste kiss, and turned smiling to face the Korians.

"Hurok and Gorah of Kor," the warrior said formally, "this is my mate, Niema.

"Is she not beautiful to behold?" he asked, grinning proudly.

Hurok admitted that she was, although privately he thought the black woman much too skinny and vastly preferred Gorah, whose proportions were ampler. But everyone to his own taste, he thought to himself.

The mating ritual of the Aziru is short and simple. By publically claiming Niema before all challengers, Zuma had married her.

It was that simple.

Tharn and his fellow chief saw to it that their people had crossed the deep crevasse and were assembled in good order on the far side. The herd of grymps had moved far off in the eastern corner of the plain and were by now too far distant to be of any potential danger to the Cro-Magnons.

At council, it was decided that the tribes should skirt the marshy borders of the swamp, circling them in order to march across the plain and reach the jungles of the south.

Long ago, at the very beginning of our adventures in the Underground World of Zanthodon, Professor Potter and I had gone by this same route into the north, when we were captives of the Neanderthal slavers from Kor. It was during this brief but irksome period of captivity that we had first made the acquaintance of Darya and Jorn, and the villainous Fumio. Hurok of Kor had been one of the warriors accompanying the slave-raid, of course, so all of these parts of Zanthodon were more than familiar to us.

Tharn regretted the absence from the tribes of my own company, although he understood and sympathized with our desire to find the missing Hurok before continuing on south to Thandar; and he was annoyed that his daughter Darya had gone back into the jungle to find Eric Carstairs.

He was reluctant to venture into the southern jungles until all of us were rejoined to the tribes.

"Let us camp on the edges of yonder jungle," he said to Garth, "within easy view of our missing friends when they emerge from the brush."

"That is agreeable to me," said Garth. "And may I suggest that it would be wise to leave the felled trees in place so as to afford an easy bridge across the abyss for them when they arrive on the scene."

Tharn of Thandar agreed that this was a sensible idea, and issued commands to his chieftains to set up camp once they had crossed the small plain, circled the swampy area, and reached the jungle's edge.

This was accomplished in very little time, and, while the scouts and huntsmen ranged afield to procure food for the meal, youths and oldsters dug fire pits in the floor of the grassy plain and women and girls constructed braces and spits from tree branches, wherefrom to suspend the hunters' kill above the coals.

After the meal was slain, cleaned, cooked and eaten, while all those not stationed on sentry-duty were bedding down for the sleeping period, Tharn stood with strong arms folded upon his mighty breast, staring with brooding eyes back across the plain and the abyss to the edges of the jungle.

There Garth and his mate, Nian, joined him.

"Is all easy in your heart, my brother?" the High Chief of Sothar solicitously inquired. Tharn nodded somberly.

"My country of Thandar lies only a few 'wakes' march to the south of these jungles," he said. "Very soon we will return to our villages and you will enter the new home of your people, and our tribes will be joined in friendship forever. It is only that I wish that Eric Carstairs and his warriors, and Darya the gomad were with us."

Garth nodded understandingly, saying nothing. He knew that Zanthodon is always full of surprises, and that in the weird subterranean cavern world, the unexpected usually happens.

They turned away to seek their rest, leaving Tharn to brood on the missing.

Chapter 22.

WHEN COMRADES MEET

"What the devil am I supposed to do with you!" repeated the Professor, and indeed it was a bit of a problem.

Baron Von Kohler regarded him thoughtfully.

"If I may ask a question, Herr Doktor," he said, "then permit me to inquire, now that the war is over and ended, are our two countries still enemies?"

Professor Potter slowly shook his head.

"No, as a matter of fact, sir, they are firm friends and allies," he said reluctantly. The German officer smiled.

"Then, since we are no longer at war with each other, cannot you and I, and the pretty *fraulein* here, emulate our governments and be, if not exactly friends—for friendship must be earned before it is returned—at least allies?"

The Professor thought it over, chewing on his moustache.

Von Kohler smiled. "After all, we are civilized white men marooned in an unknown world among primitive savages and terrible beasts, a world torn by storm and earthquake, where deadly perils are to be found on every side. Should not civilized gentlemen stand together against the common dangers with which we are so continuously beset?"

The Professor looked at him with candid suspicion.

"Your words are persuasive, and peaceable, my dear Baron," he admitted. "But it is difficult for me to decide whether they are honestly representative of the emotions within your heart, or, as seems more than likely, prompted by the fact that my spearpoint is leveled at that same organ.

"In a word, sir," he added bluntly, "I do not know whether I can trust you."

The officer nodded thoughtfully, with a charming smile. "Your caution is only common sense, I suppose," he admitted. "And were I in your position, sir, I have no doubt that I would feel the same. Well, then, what are we to do? I cannot remain long absent from my camp, for my superior is gravely injured and, before long, one of the two men under my com-

132

mand will come looking for me. If you will permit me to return to my camp, I give you my word of honor as an officer and a gentleman that I shall neither interfere with your own freedom nor attempt to molest either you or the young *fraulein*."

They both glanced at the Mauser which lay at their feet.

"I am, however, reluctant to brave the hazards of these jungles without the comfort and security of my rifle," Von Kohler added.

"I can understand that," muttered the Professor fretfully. "As I am reluctant to permit you to resume possession of the firearm, while the girl and myself have nothing wherewith to defend ourselves against you save for these flimsy spears."

"We are on the horns of a dilemma, then, as one of your English poets has so graphically put it," said the officer. "In all candor, Herr Doktor, I wish that I could think of a way in which to demonstrate decisively to you that my men and I mean you and the young lady no harm, and would in fact desire to become friends and allies with you and your people. But, alas, I have nothing but the words uttered from a sincere heart—"

At that moment someone cleared his throat behind them.

"Herr Oberlieutenant, I am here!" said a guttural voice in German. The Professor felt his heart sink into his boots, or would have, if he had been wearing any boots, which he was not.

He turned to see a second German in tattered army uniform, leveling a Mauser rifle at himself and Darya.

Heaving a gusty sigh, the old scientist let the spear drop to the ground as Von Kohler knelt and recovered his own rifle, which he snapped to safety and slung over his shoulder.

"Thank you, Schmidt, your intervention is a timely one," he said crisply. Then, turning to the old scientist, he said with equal crispness:

"And now, Herr Doktor, the conditions are reversed. How does it please you to no longer have the upper hand?"

My hunters had mostly returned with game, which we cleaned and began to cook. We had dug a fire pit in the sandy shores of the underground sea, and were relaxing when a far-off *halloo* called to our attention the return of the missing hunter, Varak.

His companions were such a surprising and a welcome sight that we sprang to our feet in delighted amazement.

"Jorn! Yualla!" I exclaimed. The two youngsters were grinning broadly as we crowded around, all talking excitedly at once. Since none of us had ever expected to see them alive and whole again, our excitement was understandable.

"Yualla," I said, hugging the smiling girl, "your father, Garth, will certainly be relieved to see you, for he long since presumed you slain by the thakdol."

"Where is my father, and our people?" she asked. I pointed into the jungles.

"The tribes are on their way south to the land of Thandar, your new home," I said. "Nor are they very far ahead, for we but recently parted from the host in order to find Hurok of Kor—"

Jorn, who had grown to love the huge, hulking old fellow during their march across the plains of the north to the range of mountains known as the Walls of Zar, grabbed my arm.

"What has become of Hurok?" he demanded. I shrugged helplessly.

"He left us during the sleep-period," I explained. "We tracked him here, to the shores of the Sogar-Jad, but can go no farther. We believe that he returned to his island homeland for some reason, but whether or not he will return to rejoin us on the mainland, we do not know."

"Have you seen Niema?" interrupted Yualla of Sothar, looking around her, hoping to see her new friend.

"Who is Niema?" I asked.

"A beautiful, tall woman," Jorn informed us, "who joined us in the mountains and captured Xask and that little villain, Murg."

"Xask and Murg, eh?" growled huge Gundar at my side. "Are those two still about?" The giant Goradian had known of Xask's villainies while a gladiator, fighting at my side in the arena of Zar during the Great Games. And he had heard tell of Murg since then. We all looked at one another with grim consternation, for while nobody had much to fear from pitiful little Murg, Xask was a wily and cunning foe, and an adversary to be reckoned with.

"Jorn forgot to tell you that Niema is black of skin," offered Yualla. My frown cleared, for now I recognized the name as that of the black woman for whom Zuma had been searching.

I opened my mouth to say as much, when the swift movement of events made my remark unnecessary.

Varak yelled excitedly, pointing with his spear. We turned

to look down the beach and saw a most welcome sight, indeed. For toward us strode a grinning Zuma with his arm about the supple waist of a stunningly handsome black woman garbed and armed as he . . . and behind them waddled the huge, hairy form of Hurok of Kor, accompanied by a smaller, slighter Korian, obviously the female of the species.

Before long we were all together again, and many tales were told and Zuma introduced us to his mate, Niema of the Aziru, while Hurok made us known to his she, Gorah of Kor.

Niema greeted us modestly, beaming with happiness at finding her beloved Zuma, but Gorah was more timid and reluctant and hung back shyly, saying little and half afraid to meet our eyes. She had seen very few of the panjani and had always been taught to regard them as her implacable enemies, and the enemies of all her kind.

For our part, however, we looked the Neanderthal woman over with frank curiosity, never having before seen a female of the race. As I have mentioned, Gorah was smaller and lighter of build than her mighty mate, and where his muscular body was thatched with matted russet fur, her skin was less hairy than his, and the fur was more downlike and silky, a lovely shade of coppery-red. It grew on her forearms to the elbow, and on her heavy thighs, and a patch grew between her shoulder-blades, while the hair on her head was heavier and longer than Hurok's. As well, her features were less crude and more refined than his, although she was certainly not to be considered handsome beside the Cro-Magnon women.

Still and all, in the eyes of Hurok she was beautiful, and, after all, that's what really mattered.

"Now we are missing only the old man, your friend, for our number to be complete once again," sighed Varak, sliding his arm around his own mate, little Ialys of Zar. I nodded grimly.

"I would have thought the old fool would have returned quite a while ago," I grumbled, "since the volcanic action has subsided long since." And it was true: an hour or so had gone by since the eruption and earthquake had shaken the jungle and split the southern plain, and still Professor Potter had not returned to our camp.

"Then it is the suggestion of Zuma that we go and find the old man," said that warrior.

By this time we had all eaten, sharing our food with the new arrivals, who were rested from their various exertions and adventures, so we broke camp, extinguished the cook-fire by raking dry sand over the glowing coals, took up our weapons and entered the jungles.

"See! Did not Varak speak the truth awhile back?" exclaimed Varak, pointing to where a crude mark had been cut in the bark of a tall cycad.

And I remembered that he had earlier predicted that the Professor would not be foolish enough to try to go through the jungle without blazing a trail so that he could find his way back to our encampment on the beach, since one part of the jungle looks so very much like every other part of the jungle, and it is easy to lose one's way therein—especially if one lacks the Zanthodonians' innate sense of direction.

"Thank heaven for small favors!" I said grumpily.

Following the trail the Professor had left, we moved swiftly through the jungle country.

Chapter 23.

THE LOST TRAIL

With a gloomy look on his face, Professor Percival P. Potter surrendered his spear and Darya did likewise, while Manfred Von Kohler stood smiling at his ease, his own rifle now slung upon one shoulder.

"Well, sir, we are your prisoners now, for the sudden appearance of your comrade has quite effectively turned the tables," said the old scientist stiffly.

Von Kohler smiled broadly and clicked his bootheels together, inclining his head in a brief nod.

"I thank you, Herr Doktor! And I must admit that this turn of events pleases me deeply, for it gives me precisely the sort of opportunity I was just wishing for."

While the Professor and Darya looked at him uncomprehendingly, the officer turned to the second soldier who stood at the far side of the glen, his rifle leveled.

"Corporal Schmidt!"

"*Ja*, Herr Oberlieutenant?"

"You will oblige me by putting up your rifle," said the officer crisply. Schmidt blinked, but obeyed, slinging the Mauser over his shoulder.

Von Kohler turned to the Professor and the Cro-Magnon princess.

"Herr Doktor, if you and the *fraulein* would likewise oblige me, you would take up your weapons again," he said.

The Professor wasted no time in stooping to snatch up his spear and Darya took up her own.

"Now you are armed again, and our firearms are across our shoulders," said the Baron. "Corporal Schmidt's unexpected appearance on the scene has granted me the very opportunity I wanted—the perfect way to prove to you and the *fraulein* that I and my soldiers wish to be your allies, not your captors or even your enemies!"

The Professor gaped.

"Well, upon my soul," he stammered helplessly. But Darya

137

proved herself quicker on the uptake than was the savant. With a warm, generous smile, she shouldered her spear and stepped forward to lay the palm of her hand lightly upon the breast of the German officer. It was the simple Cro-Magnon equivalent of a friendly handshake, the welcome to a new ally.

And the officer gallantly returned the gesture in his own way, by lifting her hand gently to his lips with a courtly bow which the jungle girl privately thought charming.

"Now that these matters have been settled," Von Kohler said, turning to Professor Potter again, "I really must return to my Colonel; I could wish that you and the *fraulein* might accompany Schmidt and me back to our camp to enjoy what rude hospitality we have to offer, but if you wish to return to your own camp, I will certainly understand, and let us part as friends, on the understanding that the world is small and we shall all doubtless meet again."

The Professor cleared his throat.

"Kerr-*hem!* Well, and as for that, we have not been absent long enough to be seriously missed, or to cause our friends to worry concerning our safety and welfare, and . . . Holy Hippocrates, sir, I have some little understanding of medicine, and feel obligated to offer your Colonel whatever help I may be able to give—"

"I am delighted to accept your kind offer, Herr Doktor! Our camp lies in that direction—Schmidt! Fall in behind to guard our rear."

And with those words, Manfred Von Kohler turned, offering Darya his hand to assist her over a fallen tree, and the four of them disappeared in the underbrush.

Xask followed Darya, the Professor, and the two Germans back to their camp in the jungle, with poor Murg whimpering at his heels. The vizier was afire with lust to get his hands on one of the thunder-weapons with which the strangers seemed so lavishly equipped. Surely, before very long, an opportunity for him to do so would present itself, for neither the Professor nor Darya knew that he was anywhere in the vicinity, and the German soldiers were not even aware of his existence.

From the cover of the underbrush between the tall trees, he and Murg observed as the party entered the camp. Yet another soldier was on guard with yet another Mauser rifle, and he clicked his heels and saluted with the weapon as the Oberlieutenant came up to him. They conferred briefly, and then

Von Kohler led his guests to the rude hut where an older, white-haired man lay on a crude litter. His garments had been torn away from his side, and a gory mass of bandages was held there by strips of cloth. It would seem that the Colonel had been gored in the side by a beast, and from the looks of him, Xask shrewdly guessed that the older man had not very long to live.

The camp was situated at the edge of a small stream, with its back against the shelter of large rocks. Bedrolls were neatly lined up beside a small fire which crackled merrily, browning plucked-and-gutted zomaks suspended above the flames on a spit made from tree branches.

While the Professor knelt to gingerly undo the wad of blood-soaked bandages and examined Colonel Dostman's injuries, Xask quickly surveyed the camp. Obviously, when the next sleeping-period came, the bedrolls would be occupied, with at least one of the Germans standing guard lest hostile natives or dangerous beasts attack the sleeping men.

Xask had no way of guessing which of the German soldiers would occupy which bedroll, but he noticed that one of the rolls of blankets was nearer to the huge rocks than were the others. He thought he could circle the camp without causing any sound, and, with a little bit of luck, creep through the boulders to purloin one of the thunder-weapons, which would doubtless be laid on the greensward beside its slumbering owner.

Finding a secure niche, he curled up on a bed of dry leaves between the enormous roots of a giant tree, and patiently awaited his chance to steal the rifle, leaving Murg to watch the camp.

For a time we followed the trail the Professor had blazed on the trees of the jungle without difficulty. He seemed to be heading directly south and east, heading straight for Fire Mountain without diverging from his path, save to go around natural obstacles.

And then, quite suddenly, the trail of marked trees ended. He went on a bit, then paused, looking around. This section of the jungle seemed no different in any way from the other parts of the jungle, and we could not at once determine the reason why the blaze marks had ended so abruptly.

"Perhaps the old man, your friend, was frightened by one of the great beasts," suggested Warza to me. I shrugged.

"Maybe, but I don't see any signs of the passage of a beast large enough to have scared the Professor into flight," I said. And indeed there were no trampled underbrush, broken branches, or footprints in the turf which would have suggested the sudden arrival on the scene of a dangerous predator.

"A vandar prowls silently, gliding through the bushes, and seldom leaves prints," Jorn pointed out. I had to agree with him, and, armed only with a spear, the Professor would certainly have taken flight before the advance of the giant sabertooth, rather than staying around to fight the cat with so flimsy a weapon.

I turned to Zuma, who, with his sharp eyes and wilderness training, was the best scout in my retinue of companions.

"Perhaps we should stay here, Zuma, while you circle about to see if you can pick up the trail of the Professor," I suggested.

The black warrior grinned. "Zuma has tracked the fleeting uld across the veldt ere this," he said without boasting, "and he has no doubt that he can find the spoor of the old man, your friend."

At his side, Niema spoke up.

"Niema will accompany her mate, for two pairs of eyes are better than none," she offered. But the male Aziru shook his head decisively.

"Niema will remain here with the other women, under the protection of the warriors," he said firmly. The black girl bridled for a moment, then smiled demurely and said that she would gladly obey her mate. Her tones were meek and I believe the amazon girl rather enjoyed being told what to do by her man. Most women do, although on this point the women's liberation movement would doubtless disagree with me, and that strongly.

Without further words, Zuma glided into the brush and was gone. He moved as silently as any Algonquin brave ever did, and was all but invisible in the jungle gloom due to the dark coloration of his skin. I felt confident that if any of us could locate the Professor's trail, it would be the black warrior.

We settled down to wait. The jungle still seemed as silent as the grave, although the earthquake and the volcanic eruption were over for hours; still the dangerous beasts remained cowering in their lair, or so it appeared. What, then, could have frightened the Professor into flight, in such haste to be gone that he stopped leaving his marks upon the trunks of the trees?

Time would tell, as it always does.

And there was nothing for us to do but wait . . . and wonder.

Chapter 24

THE THUNDER-WEAPON

Professor Potter examined the injuries of Colonel Dostman and found them as serious as Von Kohler had stated. Half delirious, the older officer was running a fever and his wounds were infected.

With the medicinal virtues of certain leaves and jungle herbs known to Darya of Thandar, which were steeped in boiling water, the Professor cleaned and dressed the Colonel's wounds. Cold, wet cloths were laid upon his brow and Darya prepared a hearty broth from cooked meat which she fed to the German officer. After a time, somewhat eased of his discomfort, the older man fell into a deep sleep, which the Professor and the Cro-Magnon princess felt would do him probably as much good as had their crude doctoring.

They joined Von Kohler at the campfire and shared the meal together, talking in low tones so as not to disturb their patient.

"I fear it would be gravely unwise to attempt to move your Colonel until 'tomorrow,'" said Professor Potter, chewing thoughtfully. By this, he meant "until after we have slept again," but Von Kohler understood his meaning without the need for explanations.

The officer nodded, saying nothing. He had already thanked his two guests in quiet tones for their assistance in tending the wounded man, and there was little more to be said. He refrained from asking their opinion as to whether or not Dostman would soon recover—probably because he felt in his heart that there was little or no hope that the Colonel would ever recover, and wished to spare his guests the painful necessity of admitting the uncomfortable fact.

Von Kohler grimly knew that very soon, perhaps within hours, the sole responsibility of command would devolve upon his shoulders. It was a sobering thought, but it had to be faced. Fortunately, during the long and weary years they had wandered through the swamps and jungles and grassy plains and mountains of the Underground World, seeking a way out of Zanthodon by which they might return again to the Upper World, he had come to know and like and trust the soldiers that had survived, and knew himself capable of their leadership.

But he had gone for so long under the command of his Colonel, that he knew he would for a time feel lost without the wisdom and experience of the older man.

The pleasures of a hot meal made them all sleepy, after the excitements and exertions of the day, so they resolved to take their rest now. In Zanthodon there are no clocks, and time is a purely subjective experience: the folk of the subterranean cavern world sleep when they are sleepy, eat when they are hungry, and wake when they have enjoyed sufficient rest, without recourse to arbitrary schedules.

"If you, Herr Doktor, and the young *fraulein*, would care to, why do you not spend this sleep-period as our guests?" Von Kohler suggested. "Private Borg will take the first guard watch, and there is no need for you to make the return journey through the jungles to rejoin your friends until you have slept."

Darya and Professor Potter agreed that this was only sensible, and were given the loan of blankets by Schmidt, who seemed in charge of the supplies. Without further ado, the elderly savant and the jungle maid curled up to either side of the campfire and fell asleep. Von Kohler strolled the perimeter of the encampment, and looked in briefly on the sleeping Colonel, before seeking his own rest. Borg stood with his rifle slung at the ready, leaning against the boulders, taking his guardpost.

Murg awakened Xask when these things eventuated, and the vizier observed the sleeping camp. He had intended to creep through the boulders, but with Borg stationed there, alert and armed and vigilant, this now seemed to the wily Zarian a risky and less than certain course of action.

Circling the encampment on careful and stealthy feet, Xask approached the rear of the small lean-to in which Colonel Dostman slumbered. The little structure was fabricated from branches tied together with thongs, with palm leaves stretched across the upper parts to afford some protection from the sudden torrential jungle rains.

Creeping up behind the rear of the flimsy structure, Xask peered through the interstices between the wooden sticks. He saw the silver-haired officer stretched out on his litter, blankets tucked about him, obviously in a deep sleep.

Propped against the side of the lean-to, stood the Colonel's rifle, a Mauser like the others. A gleam of pure greed flamed in the cunning, narrowed eyes of Xask as he discovered himself so temptingly close to one of the thunder-weapons he had for so long coveted.

This meant he would not have to attempt to steal one from the sleeping soldiers, risking discovery from Borg, but could safely purloin the Colonel's weapon from the interior of the little hut.

Xask had carried off from the debacle of the three-way battle between the savages, the corsairs and the Dragonmen of Zar, a slim, sharp knife of that peculiar reddish-silvery metal which the Professor has tentatively identified as orichalcum, the mystery metal of the fabled Atlanteans.

Drawing the blade from its sheath, he sawed stealthily at the thongs which bound the tree branches together to form the rear wall of the lean-to. Erelong, he succeeded in creating an opening large enough for his slender form to make entry. Moving with all of the cautious stealthiness of a stalking cat, the Zarian entered the lean-to and reached out to grasp the precious firearm.

The sleeping officer opened sharp blue eyes and looked at the thief!

Without a moment's thought or hesitation, Xask struck like a cobra. The Minoan dagger was still clenched in one fist; an instant later it was sunk to the hilt in the throat of the injured man, who stared up at Xask with wide, astonished eyes, which soon were closed in the final sleep of death.

Murg lurked miserably at the edge of the clearing, just behind the cover of a thick wall of bushes, whispering woefully to himself. He was, in fact, counting in the only way known to a savage race who have yet to progress farther in their mathematical computations than the number of fingers on their hands.

". . . Thakdol . . . thakdol . . . thakdol . . . thakdol," whispered the little man to himself, according to the prearranged plan in which Xask had sternly instructed him. It had been Xask's opinion that he would need a diversion to draw the attentions of the sentry from the encampment, and he had commanded Murg to count thakdols on his fingers until he had counted the sum of both hands three times over. Then he was to throw a gourd which Xask had found lying at the base of one of the palmlike trees which grew in this part of the jungle.

This, Xask presumed, would draw Borg away and give him time to enter the camp and steal one of the rifles lying beside the bedrolls of Von Kohler or Schmidt. As we have just seen, the small stratagem proved unneccessary, for at the last moment Xask had switched to a new plan, entering the hut where Colonel Dostman slept. But Murg had no way of knowing this and assumed Xask by this time to be hiding among the huge rocks at the far end of the German camp.

Counting thakdols is dreary, boring work, and it left Murg's mind free to wander among happier memories and more pleasant vistas of the imagination. The miserable little rogue heartily feared and detested Xask, who used him with casual cruelty, ignoring his feelings. Feverishly did Murg wish that Xask would never return from the German encampment, or that he would be caught, thus affording Murg an excellent opportunity to creep off into the jungle and vanish to some haven of safety which, surely, he could find in this uninhabited wilderness.

But he was afraid not to throw the gourd, fearing that Xask would return and beat him for ignoring his commands. So, when, at length, he had counted the thirtieth thakdol, the little fellow rose, hefted the hollow gourd, and flung it into the depths of the jungle where it thumped and clattered against the trunk of a tree and fell with a muffled thud to the ground.

The clattering noise came from the pebbles which Xask had inserted into the hollow gourd.

Even as Xask had expected, Borg stiffened, swiveling his eyes toward the direction from which this unusual sound had come. He strained his ears, but heard no crackle in the underbrush which would be the sign of a dangerous predator's furtive advance upon the camp. However, all in all, it would be wiser to investigate the sound, before dismissing it as harmless, reasoned Borg to himself. Charged as he was with the safety of his sleeping officers and fellow-soldier in the camp, the conscientious Borg stepped away from the rocks he had been leaning against, and crossed the clearing to peer through the trees in the direction from which the small sound had come.

The sound had been too small to arouse the sleepers, who still lay wrapped in their blankets.

Now Xask, armed with the stolen Mauser rifle, came from the entrance of the lean-to and crossed the greensward himself, after a quick and careful look at Borg, who had disappeared through the trees, having gone some little ways into the jungle.

On swift feet, Xask crossed to crouch beside one of the blanket-shrouded sleepers. His sharp eyes had, of course, noticed that Professor Potter was among the visitors to the German camp, and, next to the thunder-weapon, he most fervently desired to take captive the one man in all of Zanthodon who knew the secrets of its manufacture.

But, alas, things have a way of turning out wrong, it seems. For Xask himself had been dozing when the Professor and the others took to their rest, and, although Murg had pointed out to his master the blankets under which the Professor slept, Murg had blundered in his identification.

So, when Xask reached out to snatch away the blanket from the sleeper's face and, with the other hand, thrust the muzzle of the thunder-weapon threateningly into that face, he saw with a start of surprise that it was Darya who blinked amazedly at him from the bedroll.

Chapter 25.

MURDER!

Prowling like a hunting panther, Zuma glided on silent feet through the thick underbrush of the prehistoric jungles, every sense alert to the presence of danger. The black warrior knew no other life than this, having been born and raised in the kraal of his tribe on the edges of the jungle to the north, where it bordered upon the plain of the thantors. A trained, experienced hunter since boyhood, instructed in the arts of stalking game by the mature men of his dwindling people, Zuma knew the jungle and its ways as well as you and I know our own living rooms.

He knew the thousand small signs which indicate the perils which might lurk to every side—the snapping of a twig beneath the weight of a crouching beast, the rustling in the foliage overhead as leaves gave way to the gliding coils of a monstrous serpent, the sudden deathly silence that falls upon the jungle as the small, timid beasts huddle in trembling terror when the great predators are aprowl.

But when there came to the sensitive ears of Zuma the thump and hollow rattle of the gourd thrown by Murg when it struck the tree, the black warrior froze into instant immobility. Such a sound—slight disturbance though it was—was unfamiliar to the Aziru, and it puzzled him.

Instants later there was borne to his nostrils with the shifting of the breeze the unmistakable scent of burning wood, as from a campfire.

This was followed by a slight rustling in the bushes, as if some large and bulky form were attempting to pass through them.

Without thought, Zuma dropped his assegai and leaped into the air. Catching hold of a low bough he swung himself lightly up into the cover of the leafy branches, flung himself at full length along a broad branch and watched with keen eyes to discover what was about to appear.

The man who stepped through the wall of brush to peer

147

about was strangely clothed to the eyes of Zuma and was a stranger. The black warrior had learned from his experience with Eric Carstairs and the Cro-Magnons that white men, albeit strangers, are not necessarily to be counted as among his enemies; still and all, Zuma had not survived the perils of Zanthodon to this point in time by acting on rash, imprudent impulse. So he held his tongue and watched, and waited.

The man, whoever he was, did not seem to be a Cro-Magnon, for Zuma's experience with that race had taught him that such have invariably blue or grey eyes and yellow hair, whereas the eyes of this man were brown and his hair the grey of granite boulders. He covered his body with pieces of tan-colored cloth, clumsily and insecurely sewn together, and wore a strange piece of cloth atop his head.

Zuma had never seen a campaign cap such as those once worn by the soldiers of Rommel's famous Afrika Korps, so he could hardly have identified the item of headgear.

More to the point, the stranger bore in his hands a curious contraption made of blue-black metal, with a thick tube of the stuff at one end and a brace or stock of wood fitted to the other. Zuma knew even less of rifles than he knew of German headgear, but something in the way the apparatus was held gave the black warrior the conviction that the device—whatever it was—was a dangerous weapon.

Invisible in the gloom of the thick foliage, lying without moving a muscle or making the slightest sound, the Aziru warrior observed the stranger, taking no chances.

The stranger looked about this way and that, then went into the trees from which he emerged in a few moments, a rueful grin on his features, sheepishly regarding a dried and hollow gourd for no particular reason that the mystified black could imagine.

Then the stranger turned about and reentered the wall of bushes from which he had come.

Zuma swung lightly to the ground a moment or two later, retrieved his assegai, and stepped into the bushes to investigate.

Xask bit his tongue fiercely, to choke back an oath of anger and surprise. Any instant now, the sentry would return to the scene, having investigated the odd sound and finding nothing dangerous—which gave the vizier no time to awaken the Professor. If he tried to do so, the whole camp would be awake and upon him, as two captives are difficult to control and either of them might manage to give the alarm.

Briefly, a vicious thought flashed through Xask's mind: it would be easier to club Darya into unconsciousness or slip his blade into her, as he had done to the old German officer in the lean-to. Just as swiftly as the idea had occurred to him, the vizier dismissed it. Darya would make as good a hostage as the Professor: holding her, he could force the old scientist to surrender to him on peril of the Cro-Magnon girl's life.

He urged her to her feet with a brutal gesture. Darya silently obeyed, knowing the power of the weapon which Xask had pointed at her face. But her mind was racing with ideas as the resourceful jungle girl tried to figure a way of arousing the others without causing Xask to pull the trigger.

Alas, no idea good enough to risk her life on occurred to her at the moment.

Xask drove her at gunpoint into the trees which fringed the camping place, and urged her about the camp to the place where he had left Murg.

The little man was surprised and disconcerted to see Xask reappear with the Cro-Magnon princess, but sensibly held his tongue, rather than blurt out questions. One apprehensive look at the murderous expression on Xask's smooth features made the miserable little fellow decide wisely to restrain his curiosity.

Xask bade Murg bind the girl's wrists behind her back and gag her with a bit of cloth, which Murg hastily did.

"This way—quickly, now!" hissed Murg. And he guided his captive and his hapless accomplice into the further depths of the jungle where they vanished in the gloom.

As soon as Borg returned to the camp, he at once noticed that one of the bedrolls was unoccupied. He recalled that the Cro-Magnon woman had been sleeping there, and did not at once realize that anything was wrong. I suppose he merely assumed that the *fraulein* had sought the privacy of the bushes in order to relieve nature.

But she did not return.

Remembering that he was supposed to look in on Colonel Dostman from time to time, Borg entered the little lean-to and uttered a shocked, horrified cry which was loud enough to rouse Von Kohler from his slumbers.

Snatching up his rifle the German officer burst into the hut and stared with incredulous horror at the sight which met his eyes. The old man lay on his side, eyes open, glazed and sightless. His throat had been slit and bright blood bedabbled his bare chest.

"*Gott in Himmel!*" breathed Von Kohler, white to the lips. He knelt and swiftly examined the body, but his probing fingers found no pulse. The Colonel was dead.

He glanced up at Borg's shocked face.

"Did you see anything—anyone?" he demanded.

The soldier came to rigid attention.

"*Nein, Herr Oberlieutenant,*" he replied stiffly. Then he reported on the sound of the hollow gourd, how he had briefly left the area to investigate, and had returned to find the Cro-Magnon girl missing. Von Kohler pursed his lips thoughtfully. It seemed hardly possible that the young woman should have so brutally murdered an injured, helpless man whom she did not even know, but no other solution presented itself for immediate scrutiny. But what could possibly have been her motive for—

"*Herr Oberlieutenant,*" said Borg, licking dry lips. Von Kohler followed the direction of the soldier's pointing finger and realized that Colonel Dostman's Mauser was not in its accustomed place, propped against the side of the little lean-to. His face hardened: they had few firearms left, and precious little ammunition, so the loss of a single loaded weapon greatly reduced their ability to defend themselves against the savage tribes and ferocious monsters of the jungle.

But then his features relaxed, for his thoughtful gaze, as it strayed about the cramped interior of the small hut, discovered a further item, and that was the opening which Xask had made in the rear wall.

"The murderer entered from the rear," he breathed. "I believe the savage *fraulein* to be innocent. Whoever the man was, he must have forced her to accompany him during the few moments you were absent from the scene, investigating the source of the sound you heard, which was obviously planned to divert your attention."

Rising to his feet, he addressed the soldier.

"Rouse the camp," he said crisply. "They will not have had time to go far!"

PART SIX

———◆◆◆———

Eric of Zanthodon

Chapter 26.

XASK AT BAY

As Zuma watched from his place of concealment in the thick bushes, he observed as Xask and Murg bound and gagged Darya and led her deeper into the jungle. The black warrior frowned in puzzlement; he had never before seen Xask or Murg, or, for that matter, Darya of Thandar, and had no idea of who they might be. But, since the golden-haired girl had entered the German camp in the company of Professor Potter, he knew or hazarded a guess that she was one of the friends of Eric Carstairs.

Which meant that the two men who had forced her to go with them were her enemies, and, therefore, his own foes as well.

Zuma glided into the underbrush, following the two men and their prisoner of swift and soundless feet, wondering what to do. From the appearance of the weapon Xask carried, which was identical with the one he had seen the German soldier carrying, Zuma knew that his assegai would afford him little protection. He had never seen the so-called "thunder-weapons" used, but his imagination, built upon what he had heard in casual conversation, painted a dire and dreadful picture.

As he glided like a shadowy wraith through the jungle, the Aziru considered the options open to him. He might strike the two men down from the concealment of the underbrush, trusting to his swift, unerring aim to fell them before the weapon could be brought to bear against him, or he might circle about and appear to confront them with leveled spear, demanding their surrender.

The first plan seemed risky, as in his haste he might well injure the Cro-Magnon girl, their prisoner and hostage. The second seemed equally dangerous, as he had no clear picture of just what the thunder-weapon could do, of just how deadly it was, or what its range might be.

Zuma determined to follow and observe, and wait for the

153

time to be right, before making his attempt to free the jungle
girl.

He wished there was time to mark a trail, or some way he
could bring all of this to the attention of Eric Carstairs and
the others. But the two men were moving too swiftly through
the jungle to afford him sufficient leisure to blaze a trail; obviously, they were eager to put as much distance as possible
between themselves and the German soldiers.

Through the brush hurried the triumphant Xask, fondling
and gloating over the gleaming steel barrel of the Mauser,
with frightened little Murg panting at his heels and Darya
stumbling along at the end of her tether. Behind them, unseen in the gloomy murk of the jungle, where thick interwo-
ven boughs closed out the light of day, Zuma followed like a
watchful and avenging phantom, unknown to any.

The German officer wasted no time in rousing Corporal
Schmidt and Professor Potter from sleep, and rapidly ap-
prised them of the appalling events which had taken place
during their sleep-period. Schmidt was shaken by the murder
of the elderly Colonel, and the Professor was amazed at the
kidnapping of Darya, for he could not imagine who could
have done the deed, or why.

"What enemies do we have left?" he murmured dazedly.
"Kâiradine Redbeard and the Empress vanished quite some
time ago, and are certainly no longer in these parts; whatever
has become of them, no one knows . . . Kâiradine, I am
given to understand, conceived a violent passion for the child,
Darya, but how could he know we are here, and why would
he steal one of your rifles? He does not even know about
firearms . . . Zarys, of course, does . . . but she has never
seen anything more than Eric's .45 automatic, so how could
she know a Mauser for what it is? I must confess, my dear
Baron, that the entire affair has me baffled. . . ."

"We shall have all of the answers to these questions soon
enough," said Von Kohler shortly. "They cannot have gotten
far, whoever they may be, and the quicker we are on their
trail, the quicker we shall catch up with them. And then there
shall be an accounting, I assure you!"

Giving one of the pistols to the Professor, so that the old
scientist should not venture unarmed into the jungle, Von
Kohler ordered his men out and they stepped into the jungle.
The marks of the feet of three persons were soon found in
the mucky layer of rotting leaf-mulch and slick mud which

carpeted the jungle aisles, and one set of prints was small and dainty enough to have been made by a young woman of Darya's size and weight. The other two sets of prints seemed to be those of men.

"So there are two of them, then," muttered Von Kohler grimly. "Well, they are moving so swiftly as to be careless about leaving a trail, and we should be able to follow their prints easily enough. Borg, Schmidt—move out! *Hein!*"

With the two soldiers in the fore with weapons ready, the party plunged into the brush, abandoning their camp and its equipment and supplies in their hurry to catch the fleeing fugitives. Von Kohler was in a cold fury to work swift justice on the man who had murdered the elderly, dying Colonel in cold blood, and was willing to take a chance on their belongings remaining unmolested. He had served under the Colonel for all the years since first they had found their way down into the Underground World, and knew him to be a distinguished officer, a fair and honorable commander, a just and decent gentleman. And Von Kohler hungered to get his hands on the man who had murdered him in his sickbed.

Soon, to their considerable surprise, the soldiers found a *fourth* set of prints mingling with the three already discovered, and these were the prints of the feet of a man. From the disposition of the prints, the Baron assumed that the fourth man was not accompanying the three, but was also following them. He mentioned this to Professor Potter, who chewed upon his moustachios fretfully, finally shaking his head in mystification, unable to guess who the mysterious follower might be.

"Friend or foe, it matters little," grated Von Kohler in a harsh voice, hefting his Mauser meaningfully. "We have enough fire-power between the four of us to account for a tribe of the savages in full strength."

"Let us hope such does not prove to be the case," breathed the old scientist fervently. Then he stopped talking and saved his breath for the chase, finding it difficult to keep up with the German soldiers.

When Zuma did not return after a while, my men became restive and we decided to strike out on our own. We circled the area as we presumed the black warrior to have done, but without finding any marks left by the Professor. Obviously, for whatever reason, he had not resumed marking the trees at intervals along his way in order to blaze a trail.

Neither had Zuma, as he had expected to return to join us before having gone far enough for that to be necessary.

It was by sheer chance that we came upon the abandoned camp which the Germans had recently left. Thon of Numitor, who had sensitive nostrils, smelled burning coals and we discovered the small glade, the lean-to, the abandoned bedrolls, and the small fire which was smoldering out.

We examined the area with amazement and curiosity. The blankets were obviously of civilized manufacture, as were the cooking utensils and certain items of personal gear which had been left behind, but there was no way of identifying the origin of the mysterious items. It was a mystery . . . but I knew that other explorers besides the Professor and myself had recently penetrated into the jungles of Zanthodon. Whether they would prove friends or foes, I had no way of telling.

We pressed on, soon finding the trail of many feet in the wet mud of the forest's floor.

A warm, drenching rain began to fall.

Xask had no idea of the direction in which he was going, but something urged him to keep moving. Some sixth sense warned the wily Zarian aristocrat that vengeful armed men were on his trail, so he refused to halt for anything. If Darya stumbled over a root and fell, he jerked her rudely to her feet again and thrust her on before him. If Murg squeaked and slipped in the mud, Xask merely kicked him to his feet and forced him forward.

Abruptly, and without warning, the jungle ended and the two villains and their captives came stumbling out of the bushes to find themselves facing a broad and swampy plain.

A steamy rain was falling heavily, which made it impossible for the two men to see very far in either direction. Xask was in panicky flight by now, and kept forcing his companions along. But even he was forced to come to a halt at the brink of the deep crevasse that split the plain apart. Murg took one look at the black abyss which yawned hungrily at his feet, and fell to his knees, whimpering and snuffling piteously.

Xask stared wildly about. In the drenching downpour he could not see the fallen tree trunks which the Cro-Magnons had used to bridge the gap.

Swift as thought, an arrow whizzed from the underbrush.

It narrowly missed Xask, causing him to start and flinch violently.

From the bushes, Zuma stifled a groan of regret. The downpour had blurred his eyes, making him miss. It had been his intention to sink the arrow into Xask's wrist, forcing him to drop the weapon. But his shaft had exactly the opposite effect.

Spitting startled curses, Xask whipped the Mauser up and pulled the trigger, meaning to spray the bushes from which the shaft had flown with a deadly hail of hot lead—

Chapter 27

MURG'S WAY

When Xask gave a vicious pull on the trigger . . . nothing whatsoever happened! The thunder-weapon refused to fire, for some unknown reason of its own.*

As soon as the Aziru warrior loosed his shaft and knew that he had missed, he ducked back into the woods and sought refuge behind the thick bole of a towering Jurassic conifer, guessing that Xask would use the rifle. He hid behind the trunk, waiting for the thunderous noise he had presumed would shortly shatter the monotonous murmur of the rain. When no such sound came to his ears, he ducked from the cover of the trees to investigate.

Xask blinked incredulously at the useless piece of metal in his hands, then flung it from him with a snarling oath.

"Look!" chattered Murg excitedly, pointing. Xask gazed in the direction his slave was indicating.

The rain had lessened and the clouds were swiftly passing by overhead, driven by the gusting winds that blow through the cavern-sky of Zanthodon. As the shower died as suddenly as it had sprung up, the vizier saw the trunks the men of Thandar and Sothar had dragged across the chasm—and Xask knew he could cross the ravine to the safety of the plain, no matter who was pursuing him through the jungles.

"Quickly, Quickly!" he snapped. "We can cross to the other side and then shove the trees loose so that they will fall into the abyss and prevent our pursuers from catching up with us—"

Snatching Darya to her feet with a cruel grasp on her upper arm, he propelled the bound and helpless girl to the edge of the chasm. Turning, he beckoned curtly to Murg.

The miserable little fellow was in an agony of indecision.

---

* When it was eventually recovered, it was found that the Mauser's safety was on. Xask did not know that automatic firearms are equipped with a safety catch.

He lived in a terror of heights, remembering the heart-stopping experience of crawling down the sheer sides of the Peaks of Peril at the behest of One-Eye, when I had led the tribe of Sothar out of their captivity to the Gorpaks. And, later, he had shrunk from the dreadful necessity of scaling the mountains called the Walls of Zar by fleeing during the sleep-period from Hurok and Varak and the others into the relative safety of the northern plain.

And now he must cross—*that?*

He shuddered, gripped by a horror of the heights.

And suddenly, in a dazzling flash of realization, it came to Murg that Xask was unarmed, save for the dagger at his waist, and some distance away. He had thrown down the useless Mauser, and was armed neither with spear, trident nor bow.

Murg could flee!

As if he had read the mind of the pathetic little man, Xask sprang forward and seized him by the throat. Xask took a sadistic pleasure in having some sniveling whelp to bully and order about, as earlier he had enjoyed the company of the hapless Fumio. He did not intend to let the little man escape from his clutches; if for no other reason, Murg could be set to fetching firewood and preparing food and the other small but tiresome domestic tasks of camping in the wilderness.

"No, master—please!" shrilled the little fellow as Xask mercilessly forced him to the base of the fallen tree. His legs were trembling violently, and Murg dreaded trying to cross the abyss, knowing in his heart that he would lose his balance and fall to a horrible death in the unknown depths below.

"Crawl, like the worm you are!" snarled Xask, in a desperate agony to be across the tree-bridge and safe from pursuit on the other side.

At that moment, Zuma strode from the bushes to confront them with his leveled spear.

As Xask turned to snarl at this new adversary, Murg—pushed beyond the limits of his cowardice—found the moment for which he long had dreamed.

Stealthily, he plucked the steel dagger from the scabbard which hung at Xask's waist. The vizier turned a surprised glance over his shoulder on the smirking Murg. His lips parted for some startled query—

"It's Murg's way," giggled Murg, and stabbed him through the heart.

When the sudden rains ended, the farsighted scouts of Thandar and Sothar peered across the swampy plain to see if Eric Carstair's and his warriors had yet emerged from the edges of the jungle. What they saw surprised them more.

The towering form of a nearly naked black warrior was engaged in cutting loose the wrists of a beautiful young woman whom the watchers instantly recognized as Darya of Thandar. They raised a thunderous shout and sprinted back across the plain to her assistance.

At her feet sprawled the ungainly figure of Xask, his features forever frozen in an expression of slack-jawed astonishment. Of all the ways in which the vizier had envisioned the moment of his death—he had dreamed many splendid and heroic ends for himself—none was so base and ignoble as to be stabbed from behind by the whimpering little coward he had for so long scorned and mocked and used.

Seeing the warriors and scouts pelting in their direction, Zuma instinctively fell into a fighting crouch, leveling his assegai, knowing they could only come at him one at a time across the tree-trunk-bridge, and that they would be off-balance, lending him a superb advantage.

This advantage proved soon to be unnecessary, of course, for Darya, her hands freed by Zuma, tore the gag from her mouth and called to the warriors hastening to her assistance that the black man was a friend.

Tharn and Garth and some of them crossed over to clasp the Princess of Thandar in their arms and to inquire into her experiences. They gravely made the acquaintance of Zuma with that quiet natural dignity which distinguishes the so-called "savage" from civilized men. For his part, the noble Aziru greeted them on equal terms; he was, as the sole remaining male warrior of his tribe, of course, the chief of his own people.

When he had learned from the gomad his daughter of the events which had so recently transpired, and how Murg at the last, driven beyond endurance, had turned on Xask and stabbed him in the back, they turned to gaze about for Murg, but the little coward was nowhere to be seen.

Zuma shrugged expansively.

"The little man scuttled into the jungle like a frightened uld and vanished," the Aziru said simply. "Zuma doubts if he will ever dare show his face again before warriors."

"Let us hope so, at any rate," growled Garth, his frowning brows thunderous with wrath. Ever since the Omad of Sothar had learned how Murg had sought to ravish his daughter Yualla in her sleep, he had nursed a desire to hang the contemptible little traitor from the tallest tree.

It was about then that Professor Potter, puffing and red-faced, burst through the trees, crowing with delight at seeing Darya alive and well. Behind him, a bit more cautiously, came the Germans, with Baron Von Kohler in the lead. While introductions were being made all around, Corporal Schmidt unobtrusively picked up the Mauser which Xask had disgustedly cast to the ground. Then it was that Zuma learned that he owed his life to the fact that the vizier of Zar knew nothing of the safety-catch. . . .

It was upon this happy scene of rescue and reunion that I and all my company burst a few minutes later. We had been hard on the trail of Xask and Murg, Darya and Zuma, Von Kohler and his soldiers, wondering to whom all of these many footprints could possibly belong. We arrived on the scene just in time to share in the excitement and, also, the several explanations.

Once everything was made plain, we all crossed the abyss by the trunk-bridges and marched to the southern side of the swampy plain where the tribes lay encamped and eagerly awaiting our arrival. There, the Germans joined us in a very noisy feast of celebration, punctuated with long speeches while everybody told of their adventures.

Jorn and Yualla were the center of all eyes as they related the many perils through which they had passed and how Niema had met them in the mountains and later had captured Xask and Murg as they were creeping up on the Cro-Magnon youngsters.

The joy in the faces of Garth of Sothar and his mate Nian was wonderful to see as they welcomed their lost daughter back among the living and embraced her, kissing the tears of happiness from her glowing cheeks.

Those cheeks glowed much pinker, shortly after, when she shyly introduced them to the stalwart young Thandarian boy as the youth she desired as her mate.

Hurok introduced us to Gorah his mate, and told of his adventures in the cave country of Kor. Von Kohler briefly told something of his experiences in Zanthodon, and requested a brief leave from the feast in order to return to his encampment to recover the abandoned equipment left behind when they had pursued the stolen jungle maid and her kidnappers. He also wished to give his Colonel a decent burial beneath a cairn of rocks, so that the beasts would not disturb his rest.

Garth and Tharn dispatched a party of warriors with the Germans to assist them in these tasks. They were not absent from the feast for very long, and returned without incident.

I was a little dubious about the Germans, but their behavior had been gentlemanly and exemplary, and both Darya, and, of course, the Professor, reassured me of their desire for a friendly alliance.

"After all, my boy," said the Professor quietly, "the war has long been over."

Chapter 28

THE PROMISED LAND

Now that we had all found each other again, there was no longer any reason to delay our journey south. Murg had vanished into the jungles and no one felt inclined to search for him, although many of us wished that he could be brought before the rude, simple justice of the tribes to pay for some of the things he had done.

We never found out what became of him, for none of us ever laid eyes on the contemptible little man again. Perhaps he found a safe haven somewhere and spent the rest of his days alone; or maybe he was eaten by the beasts, we never knew. But at any rate he never bothered us again.

Concerning our journey south, it is not my intention to describe it at great length, for, to tell the truth, it was pleasantly uneventful. These jungles held no surprises for Tharn and his people, for they were familiar with them. The great predators avoided us, apparently unwilling to challenge so great a host of armed men. A few more "wakes" and "sleeps," and the journey proved over.

We came out of the jungle rather abruptly, to find ourselves gazing upon the land of Thandar at last. It was a broad and vast valley, a place of rolling green hills and grassy fields, laced with many small streams of fresh water and grown, here and there, with patches of forest.

It was a goodly land to look upon, basking under the eternal afternoon light of Zanthodon. Far to the east, where the woods thickened into an imposing array of timberland, a herd of thantors, or wooly mammoths, grazed peaceably, much too distant to be a cause of trouble to us.

You can perhaps imagine the emotions that passed through the hearts of Tharn and Darya and the others as they looked once again upon their homeland, after the long, weary months of wandering through strange new lands filled with enemies and perils and vicissitudes of every kind.

Tharn searched the far reaches of the wooded valley with keen eyes; then he lifted an arm to point across the plain.

"There!" he said with immense satisfaction in his tones.

We looked in the direction he had indicated, and saw a large settlement of wooden huts walled about with a palisade of logs sharpened at the top. The lazy spirals of smoke from cook-fires ascended into the serene afternoon skies. We could even see a small band of hunters returning with the morning's kill slung on poles, and women bathing in a shallow stream behind the town.

Garth and his mate Nian looked the scene over with pleased expressions on their faces.

"It looks to be a goodly land, this Thandar of yours, my brother," he remarked to Tharn, who grinned.

"Of *ours*, my brother!" said the High Chief. And Garth nodded thoughtfully, for of course he and all his people were henceforward to share the land with the first tribe. There looked to be land enough and room enough for all. . . .

Von Kohler and the two soldiers under his command studied the country through binoculars. The Germans had come with us, of course, having nowhere else to go. And Zuma and his new mate, Niema, had come with us as well. They had all become members of my company, which by this time was a catch-all for homeless foreigners, you might say.

Beside me, Professor Potter stood, a vague, dreamy look in his watery blue eyes. He tugged at my arm.

"Eric, my boy," he breathed tremulously, "do you realize what gifts we can bring to these people, you and I? We can teach them the principles of agriculture, so that no longer need they spend their days as wandering nomadic hunters; they can transform that little town into a city, and we will have helped our distant cousins, the Cro-Magnons, along the path to civilization . . . why, we can teach them brickmaking and stone masonry, so that they can build with permanence . . . we can record their language and instruct them in a simple alphabet, so that their traditions and histories can be recorded for all time, not merely handed down from generation to generation by oral means alone . . . the rudiments of mathematics should be useful to them. . . ."

Von Kohler was listening to the Professor's rambling and ecstatic monologue. He coughed apologetically and interrupted the discourse.

"Herr Doktor, I quite agree. But, do you suppose, we could perhaps avoid teaching them any of the skills or vices that have been the ruination of so many cultures? For example, the use of currency . . . money being the root of all evil, as the Scriptures tell us. Doubtless, the Cro-Magnons employ a simple barter system, exchanging skills for skills, the tanner giving his wares to the huntsman for fresh meat, the carpenter building a hut for the fisherman in return for a load of fish, and so on."

The Professor mulled it over, tugging on his stiff white moustaches.

"I suppose you are right, Baron," he said. "Money leads to usury, to greed, to the exploitation of labor . . . perhaps we can find a way to keep the Thandarians from inventing it . . . an interesting little problem in social dynamics!"

The idea of helping our Cro-Magnon friends toward civilization was beginning to get me interested, too.

"Once we have the alphabet," I said, "we can codify their tribal customs and traditions into laws, written down and mutually understood and agreed upon, if necessary by a popular vote."

Von Kohler and the Professor agreed that this was a good idea.

The Professor wandered off to talk to Tharn. Von Kohler turned to me.

"Would it not, Herr Carstairs, be a worthy cause to devote our lives to, if we could spare the Cro-Magnon nation the mistakes that have marred the history of our own Western civilization? Extreme nationalism, imperialism, the exploitation of less advanced peoples, the creation of poverty and slums, military agression . . . and, instead of these, teach them the ways of justice, equality, fairness, decency, toleration, brotherhood, cooperation, and—freedom!"

"It would indeed, Von Kohler," I said thoughtfully. "It would be our way of making up for the sins we have contributed to. Not at all a bad thing to spend the rest of your life doing. . . ."

And so we went down into Thandar, and I came home.

The settlement was more primitive than I would have expected, and dirtier and noisier. Within the palisade wall, which was broken by three gates, stood about sixty one-story huts, not counting sheds and lean-tos. These were arranged with no system, just rambling clusters, and there was nothing like streets between them, just pathways of naked earth, beaten smooth by many feet.

The sanitation system consisted of a stream which ran behind the town and which was used indiscriminately by everyone. Some of the huts, far enough away from the stream for its use to be impractical, used ditches dug behind them for the same purpose. Flies and garbage were everywhere. And it stank abominably!

Now, the Cro-Magnons were a healthy and very cleanly people, despite the conditions in the settlement. After all, Paris and London in the Middle Ages were a lot dirtier, and probably stank even more terribly. Still and all, it looked as though our friends could use the advice of some city planners like the Professor and me. Well, that was one of the problems we would have to tackle later: there was going to be enough to keep us busy for years to come.

When we came into sight, the Thandarians came out to greet us, and the welcome was enthusiastic, to say the least. Tharn strode into the gates of his town like a Caesar returned from the Gallic Wars, and he looked every inch the king that he was.

It seemed—I had never bothered to think about it before, but it would have had to be this way—it seemed, I say, that when the Drugar slavers carried off Darya and the rest of the hunting party, and Tharn pursued in strength, he left behind in Thandar a considerable number of able-bodied men, all of the women and old people and children. It would have been madness to march away with every healthy male capable of hefting a spear, leaving his homeland unprotected. No, about seventy warriors and huntsmen had been left to guard the village and do the hunting, and the reunion was glorious to witness. Warriors, absent for months on the expedition, were tearfully greeted by their mates and parents and children.

I had not realized that my warriors, Parthon and Ragor, had mates and children, for in my company they had never mentioned their existence. But, then, this is only natural: most of the time we were together, we were too busy fighting against beasts or human adversaries, or running away from same, to have much time for casual chit-chat.

Ragor's mate, a buxom, merry-faced wench named Oona with a fat baby straddling each ample hip, greeted me happily—happily, that is, because I had brought her man home again, alive, and in one piece.

"Ragor will not have had a decent meal since he left Oona," she said disapprovingly, poking a thumb in his ribs. "Look at you! All skin and bones! Well," and here she turned to grin at me, "tonight there will be a feast to end all feasts, and we womenfolk will begin putting some meat back on the bones of you helpless men!"

Chapter 29.

"BABE" FLIES AGAIN

And, that night, there was a feast, indeed! The women turned spits over beds of blazing coals, roasting succulent uld and gamey zomaks, and huge slabs of mammoth steak, and broiled huge, leathery-skinned eggs of the drunth, which were, to the Cro-Magnons, a gourmet delicacy.

We all gorged splendidly on smoking meat, and the broiled eggs alluded to above, as well as stews of juicy roots and wild vegetables, seasoned with scraps of meat and boiled into a tasty broth, and wild fruit and nuts and berries . . . and washed this huge repast down with gourdfuls of the heady native beer the Thandarians had learned to brew—or "nut-brown ale," as the Professor called it.

One by one we took turns recounting our adventures, and, as you can imagine (if you have read this book and the four other volumes of these memoirs), there was very, very much to be told, and the telling consumed many hours.

It was during these recitals, that I came to know many of the details of the adventures that happened to such of my friends as Jorn and Yualla, Hurok and Darya, Tharn and others, which I have inserted into these books in their proper place. Much, much more was learned from subsequent conversations with my comrades, and the piecing together of threads of narrative into a cohesive and comprehensive whole. It took a lot of work to figure out what had happened to everybody, but at length it was all straight in our minds.

The Thandarians were hospitable to the strangers of the Sothar tribe, and warmed to them in friendly fashion, as soon as they grasped how willingly the Sotharians had stood and fought shoulder to shoulder with their people on many occasions. It took them a little longer to make friends with Hurok and his hairy mate, Gorah, or with the two black Aziru, or the Germans.

In time, I am happy to say, everybody was friends with everybody else.

I guess we had taught the folk of Thandar something about brotherhood and tolerance already!

After the feast and the various narratives, there came a more solemn but no less joyous event. Or sequence of similar events, perhaps I should say.

I refer to the wedding ritual.

Before the combined tribes, young Jorn proudly claimed the blushing and beautiful Yualla as his mate.

Before the tribes, Varak repeated his claim to Ialys of Zar, and Grond of Gorthak took shy little Jaira as his mate.

Rituals similar in nature were repeated between Hurok of Kor and Gorah, and between Zuma the Aziru and the lovely Niema.

And then it was my turn!

Feeling absurdly nervous, I stood up with Darya smiling demurely at my side, and claimed her as my own before the presence of them all. Tharn, her father, gravely placed her hand in mine, holding both of our hands briefly in the grip of one huge hand, to signify that he gave the gomad to me to be my own Princess.

Then, while my warriors shouted and yelled our names, I stood there grinning sheepishly, feeling like a fool, while the women of my company pelted the two of us with flowers.

We shared our first kiss as mates, and the ritual was over and done.

And I felt very much married. . . .

The honeymoon is a new custom which Darya and I introduced to the Cro-Magnons of Thandar. We went into the wilderness for a week or so, and I built a little hut beside a stream in the cozy circle of a copse of Jurassic conifers. I carpeted the floor of the hut with armfuls of fragrant grasses, and for a time we stayed apart from our people, enjoying the nuptial privacy of our honeymoon.

I hunted at day and brought my kill back to my mate for her to prepare and cook. It was like something from the first ages of mankind on the earth . . . like a memory of the Garden of Eden.

And it was certainly very much like Paradise to my darling wife and me. . . .

A few days after Darya and I terminated our idyll and returned to the settlement, to take up residence in the "town hall" or royal palace of Thandar (a rather well constructed, two-story wooden edifice used as the residence of the High Chief and his family, and for judgments and ceremonial occasions), the Professor and I went on a brief, nostalgic expedition.

We took along my two giant friends, Gundar of Gorad and Hurok of Kor, for protection. These are the two most gigantic warriors I know, and with them at our backs, the Professor and I would safely have faced down half a herd of dinosaurs.

We trekked due west of Thandar, crossed the plains and entered the jungles. After a time, the jungles gave way to swampland and muddy fens; beyond, the placid surface of the Sogar-Jad glittered under the dim golden skies of Zanthodon.

We were looking for a little hilly promontory which thrust from the mainland on the shores of the subterranean sea.

We were looking for the very spot on which Professor Potter and I had first stepped forth upon the soil of the Underground World. . . .

Well, after a few days of wandering around, we reached the location we had determined to revisit. Directly overhead, like a circular and stationary dark cloud in the glowing heavens of Zanthodon, was the opening which led to the surface of the earth.

We found what remained of my faithful helicopter, Babe, by which we had long ago descended into the crater of the extinct volcano in the Sahara. She had crashed on landing, had Babe, and still lay where she had fallen, although now vines and bushes had grown thickly about her until she was almost buried in the foliage.

We cleared away the overgrowth, the four of us, and looked her over. One of her vanes was bent, and her undercarriage was crushed, and the door hung at a crazy angle on broken hinges. Aside from these unfortunate facts, she looked surprisingly whole and sound.

Dead leaves had been blown into the cabin, and a brace of zomaks had nested there, befouling the controls with their lime-white droppings. I cleaned the cabin out and checked the dials.

"You know, Doc," I said in surprise, "if we fixed the bent vane and repaired the undercarriage, and cleaned out the engine . . . I bet Babe could fly again!"

"Really?" He sounded more than a bit skeptical. "And where do you expect to buy gasoline in this world of cavemen and dinosaurs?"

"Don't you remember how many tins of gas I loaded her up with before we left the coast?" I returned. "Well, plenty of them are still full, for all the long way we flew . . . and they're still sealed, too. They haven't even sprung a leak."

He played with his little tuft of chin-whiskers, looking thoughtful.

"Perhaps it could be done, after all . . . the Thandarians have only recently entered the first crude stages of metalworking, but there is iron ore in those hills to the south, or I'm no geologist! What an impressive means of defense your helicopter would be, if ever Thandar was invaded by an enemy . . . why, there would be no need to fight at all, all you would need do is fly over the enemy ranks at a low altitude—they would bolt in every direction like chickens in a henyard, when a hawk swoops low. . . ."

I nodded. "Yep! And, with the chopper, it would be an easy thing to chart and map the extent of Thandar and the surrounding countries."

"We could even return to the surface again," he mused to himself.

"I suppose we could, Doc, but—hey! I just got married, if you'll kindly remember. I'm not about to fly off and leave my blushing bride!"

"Someday, however, we must go back, Eric my boy," he said seriously. "The data and observations I have gathered here, not only my eyewitness descriptions of the great beasts, but what I have learned about the traditions and customs of the Cro-Magnons, the Neanderthals, even the people of Minoan Crete—all of this information is of inestimable scientific value. It *must* be made available to the Upper World!"

"Someday," I agreed. But I privately thought to myself that it might not be necessary: Babe was equipped with a shortwave radio, and it looked to be still in one piece, although by now we would have to recharge the batteries, somehow. And I have a niece in upstate New York, on a farm near Lake Carlopa, who has a receiving set I built for her, tuned to the wavelength of Babe's radio. Couldn't we, someday, transmit the whole fantastic story of our adventures in Zanthodon to Jenny? Even if nobody believed a word of our story, it would sure make a heck of a series of Stone Age adventure stories for some paperback publisher like Ace or Ballantine or DAW....

To make the story shorter, we resolved to try it! Gundar and Hurok felled trees with their axes and trimmed the twigs and branches from the logs. Then they dragged them to where Babe squatted on its crushed landing gear. With leathern thongs and ropes fashioned by weaving tough, long reeds and grasses together in a sort of braid, we fastened the logs into a crude sledge.

Babe was too heavy to be dragged back to Thandar, but the Professor worked out a clumsy set of wheels which we had to keep greased with the cooked fat of zomaks I brought down with my bow. The Professor was delighted with his contrivance, but Hurok and Gundar stared at it in bewilderment, scratching their heads and exchanging mystified glances.

I guess the Professor had every right to be proud. After all, he had just invented the wheel!

It wasn't a month later before we had Babe back in good working order—and she *flew,* the first flying machine ever in the long history of the Underground World.

The grown-ups of the tribes were shaking in their boots (well, you know what I mean!) at the unearthly noise and shuddersome fact of her uncanny flight. But the kids were tickled pink!

Hurok and Gundar firmly but politely refused to accept a free ride in the chopper. Even Von Kohler looked dubious— he had vaguely heard of autogyros, but a modern Sikorsky looked too risky, too flimsy, to his eyes.

Jorn was the only one who would go up with the Professor and me, and he had to be dared into it by Yualla. The adventure-loving kid was dying to go, but I put my foot down and said no: she was carrying their child and I didn't think it would be smart to run the risk.

Anyway, Thandar's air force was born.

Chapter 30

THE OMAD-OF-OMADS

After Jorn and Yualla had their baby, little Eric, a rash of births increased our numbers. Hurok became a proud father when Gorah his mate produced a set of twins; they named the male Tor and the she they called Ungala. Also, Zuma and Niema had a daughter, an exquisite, happy, laughing, bright-eyed child they called Azira, after the founder of their tribe. She was going to grow up into as stunningly beautiful a young woman as her mother, and I'll place a bet right now that the young Cro-Magnon hearts of her teen years will be breaking to right and left.

Varak fathered a daughter too, a tiny, elfin creature that took more after his mate than after himself with the olive skin of Ialys and the golden hair of Varak—a striking combination.

The German soldiers, Borg and Schmidt, both married Cro-Magnon women and fathered sons, but Von Kohler remained single. Perhaps he was too busy working on his plans for the town (you could no longer call it a camp or even a settlement, not with its new walls of cut and mortared stone and its straight streets and decent sanitation). The Baron had studied civil engineering in his university years, before joining the army, and took charge of the new buildings which began to be erected in place of the ramshackle huts of old.

The Professor, on the other hand, was our expert on metal-working and agriculture. He discovered edible roots and primitive vegetables he believed could be cultivated into something close to potatoes and carrots, and he also experimented with various grains and cereals, finding one plant which resembled prehistoric maize and another he believed to be wheat or barley.

He laid out the cultivated fields, watered by a system of irrigation ditches, and we were soon feasting off bread that was not at all untasty. This, of course, reduced the dependence of the Cro-Magnons upon hunting for food, and gave them more leisure to work at the rebuilding of the town, which was mostly to be constructed of sun-dried or oven-baked bricks, and the hoeing and planting of the fields.

All of this became practical, even possible, only after Professor Potter found the veins of iron ore in the hills which he had suspected were there. Now that the smiths could make the proper tools, the tribes advanced at a single step to the Iron Age, to agriculture, and to urban civilization.

My own modest contribution to the march of progress consisted of the domestication of the uld. If "domestication" is quite the word I want: what I mean is, we came to collect the uld into herds and to pen them in, rather than doing it the old-fashion Cro-Magnon way and trotting across the plains with bow and arrow or spear, hoping to find a fat uld and to make a kill.

Oh, yes; another contribution—not to the march of progress, exactly, but at least to the size of my ever-growing "tribe" . . . my mate presented me with a strong, lusty infant son whom I named Gar, after my father. . . .

To celebrate the birth of our son, Tharn of Thandar and Garth of the Sotharians summoned the tribes to an enormous feast, with Darya and little Gor and me the principal guests of honor.

After the feast, Tharn rose to his feet to make a speech. For the occasion, he was rigged out in full ceremonial regalia, as befitted a Cro-Magnon High Chief: headdress plumed with zomak feathers, his necklace of sabertooth tiger fangs, bracelets and bangles of copper ornaments—the works.

"We are met here," he began in solemn tones, "to consider how properly to honor Eric Carstairs for his many services to the tribes of our people." And I felt my face turning red, for I had thought little Gar would be the center of attention, not myself. He went on:

"All of us owe very much to Eric Carstairs, and more than a few among us owe our very lives to him, to his courage, his strength, his wise counsels, his leadership, and his common sense. He came among us as a stranger from a far land, but he has earned our respect and admiration, our affection and our love. Was it not Eric Carstairs who enabled Jorn and Darya the gomad to escape from the captivity of the Drugars, and Eric Carstairs who slew Uruk, High Chief of Kor, and Eric Carstairs who led the escape to freedom of the Sotharians, from their vile slavery to the Gorpaks of the cavern city, and Eric Carstairs who brought about the destruction of the Scarlet City? It was none other than he.

"My brother Garth and I have long considered what honor to bestow upon this man, our friend. Already, he has become a chieftain of Thandar, and now his warriors have grown in number so as almost to constitute a third tribe, as oft in jest they are wont to refer to themselves. In the beginning they were seven, with Eric Carstairs and the Professor at their head—Jorn the Hunter, Parthon, Warza, Varak of Sothar, Erdon and Ragor, and Hurok of Kor. From of old, chieftains of Thandar have led seven warriors into battle, and seven only.

"But, in the course of many wanderings and adventures, to that number were joined yet others, strangers from other tribes and far lands, such as Grond of Gorthak and Jaira, and Varak's mate, Ialys of Zar, and Gundar the Goradian, and Thon of Numitor. And, more recently, Zuma the Aziru and his mate Niema, and Hurok's mate, Gorah, and Von Kohler and Borg and Schmidt. Add to this, the mates and children of the warriors, among the which is my own daughter, Darya, and the newborn among them, and you will find that those who follow Eric Carstairs as their chieftain are now many times the number of warriors that follow a mere chieftain."

Tharn was right, of course. I did some mental addition, and came up with a grand total of *forty-one!*

"It is the decree of the two tribes that we now consider ourselves three, and that Eric Carstairs shall be known in his own right as an Omad, to share our councils on equal footing and with equal voice and authority with Tharn and with Garth."

His expression became brooding, his voice sank to low tones to which all strained to hear in the dead silence.

"The tribe of Thandar was founded by my ancestor, the High Chief Thandar; the tribe of Sothar was founded by Sothar the High Chief, the ancestor of my brother Garth. But we deem it not wise, in this instance, to follow the old ways, for among the new ways that Eric Carstairs and the Professor and Von Kohler are teaching us are many that are good. Already, the tribes are become the mightiest nation known in all of Zanthodon, since the Drugars of Kor were reduced, and the Barbary Pirates decimated, and the strength of the Scarlet City of Zar destroyed. In time, our people will come to dominate all of Zanthodon, but that will be in the time of

Eric Carstairs or his sons, for by then Tharn of Thandar and Garth of Sothar will have joined their ancestors in another life.

"Let us therefore call the tribe of which Eric Carstairs is Omad, the tribe of Zanthodon. . . .

"And there is yet more! My only surviving child is my daughter, Darya the gomad, and when I am gone is not her mate, Eric Carstairs, to lawfully inherit the Omadship of Thandar? And likewise my brother Garth will be succeeded to the Omadship by Jorn the Hunter, the mate of his only surviving child, the gomad Yualla. But, as these are among the people who follow Eric Carstairs as their Omad, shall not he, too, inherit the Omadship of Sothar?

"It is so, and it can only be thus, for such are the ancient traditions which have now become the written law of our kind.

"Therefore, I hail my son-in-law and brother Omad, Eric Carstairs . . . Eric of Zanthodon . . . who will become, in times yet to be, the Omad-of-Omads, the ruler of Zanthodon itself."

And the silence was split by a roar of approval such as I have never heard, and never thought to hear. . . .

I rose to my feet, crimson to the ears, and stammered something awkward and inane, which I have long since mercifully forgotten, then bade the feast continue, and sat down again by my wife. But not before Garth and Tharn ceremoniously placed the ridiculous plumed headdress of an Omad on my brows, and clasped a necklace of sabertooth fangs about my throat, in token of my new royal rank.

Seated again by the side of my beloved Darya, I took little Gar on my lap and let him play with the gleaming ivory fangs. Tharn and Garth are both in the full noontide of their magnificent prime, and will rule for many, many years to come.

But someday the little child on my knee will be the Omad-of-Omads . . . Emperor of the Underground World.